Far

Winner of the Bisto Book of the Year Award

'A fascinating story.'
RTE Guide

'Based on the Dublin author's research into the real
Jewish refugee farm in Millisle set up during the war,
the book is a moving story of courage, prejudice and
the ability of young people to cope with the most
difficult challenges.'
Ulster News Letter

'Every young adult should read this book. It is
history, written with the gripping reality of fiction.
It is a story which, like Anne Frank's diary, brings
home to us all the horrific misery inflicted by the
Nazis – and the need to ensure that we never
allow it to happen again.'
*Lord Janner, QC, Chairman,
Holocaust Educational Trust*

MARILYN TAYLOR graduated in economics from University College London. She is married with three grown-up children and currently works in a Dublin college library. She has written three successful novels for young adults: *Could This be Love? I Wondered, Could I Love a Stranger?, Call Yourself a Friend?* Marilyn is also a founder member of Children's Books Ireland and has participated in Books Across the Border, a series of cross-border and cross-community children's book events.

FARAWAY HOME

MARILYN TAYLOR

THE O'BRIEN PRESS
DUBLIN

For Hannah, for later

First published 1999 by The O'Brien Press Ltd,
20 Victoria Road, Dublin 6, Ireland.
Tel: +353 1 4923333; Fax.:+353 1 4922777
E-mail: books@ obrien.ie
Website: www.obrien.ie
Reprinted 1999, 2000, 2001.

ISBN: 0-86278-643-6

British Library Cataloguing-in-Publication data
A catalogue record for this title is available
from the British Library

4 5 6 7 8 9 10
01 02 03 04 05 06 07

The O'Brien Press receives
assistance from

the arts
council
an chomhairle
ealaíon
50ᵗ

Editing, typesetting, layout, design: The O'Brien Press Ltd.
Cover separations: C&A Print Services Ltd.
Printing: Cox & Wyman Ltd.

Come away, O human child,
To the waters and the wild ...
For the world's more full of weeping than
   you can understand.

W.B.Yeats

CONTENTS

PART ONE

Anschluss!
Karl & Rosa: Vienna, 1938

1

Anschluss!

Karl Muller looked down from the window of his family's apartment, high on the fifth floor, to a scene unlike anything he had witnessed in all his thirteen years.

'Victory to the German Reich! ... Sieg Heil! ... Jews out!'

The raucous shouts floated up to the curtained window behind which, hidden from view, the Muller family crouched. Below in the Vienna streets, green army lorries thundered past, packed with steel-helmeted soldiers who sat stiff and motionless, clasping machine-guns. Uniformed motorcyclists zoomed by in formation, churning the sprinkling of late snow to a dirty slush. Huge blood-red flags with black swastikas, the Nazi symbol, swayed and rippled.

The cries redoubled. 'One Reich, one people, one leader ... Anschluss!'

In a sudden hush, broken by the peal of church bells, an open-topped car drove slowly down the centre of the road. In it, erect, right arm outstretched in the Nazi salute, stood the Nazi leader of Germany, Adolf Hitler.

Karl, with his parents and his little sister Rosa, watched

silently as an animal roar erupted from the crowd. Could this really be the man who was taking over their city, their country? This ordinary little man, with a ridiculous moustache, turning to left and right like a mechanical doll?

Despite the heat from the tiled stove, Karl felt suddenly cold. Hugging his dog, Goldi, he gazed over the red-tiled rooftops and slender church spires, to the Prater funfair. He had visited the fair countless times, whirling round on the giant Ferris wheel with its view over Vienna, stuffing himself and Rosa with ice cream while the grown-ups listened to the band. At home and at school, his life had been ordinary, uneventful, sometimes boring.

But now the unthinkable had happened. The Nazis had taken over Austria. They called the take-over the Anschluss. What was it going to mean, Karl wondered – to him, and to everyone around him?

Rosa tugged at her father's jacket. 'Papa, what are they shouting?' she asked. 'I want to join the parade. I'm wearing my dirndl.' She twirled to show off her coloured skirt and embroidered blouse, the Austrian national dress she liked to wear.

Her father patted her head. 'No, darling,' he answered slowly. 'We can't join in. They don't want us.'

As Rosa, disappointed, turned to her mother, a dazzling flash of light from below forced them all to step back from the window.

'What's that?' asked Rosa, her hands over her eyes.

'They're flashing mirrors up to blind us,' said Papa. 'Maybe they don't want us to see their beloved Hitler.'

'Surely not,' said Mama. 'How could they know which are our windows?'

'The ones without Nazi flags, I suppose,' said Papa. 'You know Jews aren't allowed to display the swastika. As if we'd want to!'

'Those people screaming down there can't be ordinary Austrians,' said Mama. 'Our friends and neighbours–'

'No?' Papa replied bitterly. 'People seem to have forgotten decency, justice–' He drew a handkerchief from his pocket and blew his nose. 'Overnight, they have become supporters of Hitler and his bully-boys.'

'But Papa, aren't there people who are against the Nazis?' asked Karl.

Papa shrugged hopelessly. 'The Social Democrats? They're probably hiding away in their homes, like us.'

Karl had never seen his father like this, bitter and sad. He longed for the reassuring tones Papa had always used when he was a little boy, with little problems and fears. But this – the Nazi parade, the swastikas, the hysterical screaming – was a problem that even Papa was powerless to deal with.

Karl felt as if somewhere, deep in some hidden place, a sleeping monster had stirred and was beginning to wake.

◆ ❖ ◆

Karl and Rosa's grandmother appeared from her bedroom, pulling a lacy shawl around her. 'What's happening out there? It's so noisy ...' She tucked her long grey hair into a knot at her neck. 'Why are you all hiding behind the curtains?'

'It's a parade,' Rosa told her importantly. 'But we can't be in it, Oma.'

'It's Hitler's victory parade, to mark the Anschluss,' said Mama matter-of-factly. But Karl could hear a tremor in her voice. 'It must be nearly over now.'

'I don't understand,' said Oma. 'Isn't there going to be a vote about us joining with Nazi Germany?' Her eyes, which her diminishing sight had turned a pale milky blue, were bewildered. 'I thought a lot of people were going to vote against it – there were posters everywhere, and signs painted on the footpaths–'

'That vote isn't going to happen.' Papa led her to the settee. 'Our spineless government caved in to Hitler's bullying and cancelled it. Now Germany has taken us over, and we're under Nazi rule.'

Nazi rule. With a chill, Karl remembered his father reading aloud the news from Nazi Germany – Jews beaten and attacked, driven from their homes, sent to prison camps.

'But this isn't Nazi Germany,' said Oma. 'Our Austria is a country that cares for all its citizens, whatever their religion.'

'Suppose the Nazis change things–' said Karl anxiously.

A knock at the door made them jump. Papa rose. Mama hurried in from the kitchen. 'Don't answer,' she hissed. 'It might be the Nazis, come for us.'

They all stood frozen, waiting.

There was a second knock, still soft.

'If it was them, they would bang on the door and shout,' whispered Karl. 'And look at Goldi.' She was standing quietly, waving her bushy tail.

Papa opened the door a crack. 'It's all right,' he said. 'It's only Rudi.'

Everyone brightened at the sight of Uncle Rudi, Papa's younger brother, smart in his camel hair coat.

'I had to come,' said Rudi. Karl could see that his uncle, an actor usually full of jokes and chatter, was making an effort to sound solemn. 'On such a day, the family should be together.' Rudi embraced his elderly mother tenderly and greeted the family. As soon as Rosa ran to him, he became his old self, swinging her up in his arms. 'And how's my favourite niece?'

Giggling, she patted his luxuriant chestnut hair and curly moustache. 'I'm your *only* niece, Uncle Rudi,' she said as he set her down. 'Did you see the parade?'

'I heard it on the radio,' he said. He turned to Papa. 'They're welcoming Hitler and the Nazis like saviours.'

'You heard what they're shouting about Jews?' asked Papa.

Rudi shrugged. 'It will pass,' he said. 'Our history is full of these troubles, and we're still here.'

Mama, glancing around at the solemn faces, said briskly, 'I think we should forget the Nazis and eat. Come, Oma.'

But, Karl thought, how could you forget the monster, nameless and terrifying, that was out there in the once safe and familiar streets of their city?

2

The Iron Ring

Rudi switched on the radio, which sat, squat and square, on the polished sideboard. '... children are strewing flowers along the route of his car. The people of Ostmark are full of love and admiration for our leader, Adolf Hitler, himself an Austrian ...'

'Ostmark?' said Karl. 'What's that?'

'It's the new Nazi name for Austria,' grunted Papa.

The voice on the radio spoke reverently, excitedly. 'Germany and Ostmark, united, will go forward to a glorious future, destroying our enemies–'

Papa switched it off. 'Mark my words, ours is the first country Nazi Germany has swallowed up, but it won't be the last. And when Hitler has all Europe in his power, he'll set about destroying those he hates – Jews, Gypsies, Socialists, and everyone who defies him.'

'You're such a pessimist,' said Uncle Rudi, putting his arm affectionately around Papa. 'I tell you, the Nazis won't last.' He ran his hand through his untidy hair with an actor's casual gesture. 'At the theatre, everyone thinks that man's a joke.'

He leapt to his feet; laying one finger across his upper lip, he extended the other arm stiffly and strutted up and down the small living-room in an imitation of Hitler. Goldi, think-ing this was a new game, trotted after him, barking.

Karl laughed, but Papa remained serious. 'You make a joke out of everything, Rudi,' he said. 'But the Nazis are no joke. What happened in Germany could also happen here.' He stopped as Rosa appeared from the kitchen, carrying a platter of warm rye bread.

Uncle Rudi said, a little too heartily, 'Something smells wonderful.'

As the family sat round the heavy oak dining-table, it seemed to Karl that Papa's and Uncle Rudi's words still hung in the air like a chilling echo, not quite concealed by the family laughter and argument   Papa praising Mama's feather-light potato dumplings, Uncle Rudi waving his arms about as he talked, and Goldi, her tail thumping hopefully, waiting beside Rosa's seat for bits of salami.

They all tried to ignore the occasional shouts and snatches of Nazi marching-songs that could still be heard from outside. Instead, Uncle Rudi told them about his part in a new comedy at the Burgtheatre; and Oma repeated the familiar story of how, in the Great War, the Austrian army had awarded her husband, Karl's grandfather, the Iron Cross for his courage in rescuing a wounded man from the mud of the trenches. 'I was proud of your dear Opa, but so worried about him. He came back a changed man. They called it shell-shock.' She paused, remembering. 'It was a terrible, needless war.'

'Tell us the story of the ring, Oma,' begged Rosa.

Oma put down her knife and fork. 'Well, darling, during that war the government asked all women to give gold and jewellery to help our country's war effort. You know we only had the small shoe shop which your Papa runs now, so I gave the most precious thing I had.' She lifted her hand. 'My gold wedding ring, that your Opa had worked and saved for.'

'Didn't you get it back, Oma?' asked Rosa, knowing the answer.

'No, darling,' said Oma. 'They gave us rings of iron in exchange.' She held out her claw-like hand, the iron ring loose on her bent finger.

As they ate and talked, Karl felt his earlier icy fear recede in the warmth and security of the family meal. After lunch, perhaps he would go round and have a game of football with his cousin Tommy, or visit Lisl, his closest friend. She and Karl had always told each other everything, and it had never mattered that she was Christian and he was Jewish.

Maybe Uncle Rudi was right, he told himself, the Nazis would disappear, the unnerving cheering and jeering would stop, and life would return to normal again.

◆ ❖ ◆

They were still at the table when they heard violent banging. Goldi raced to the door, barking. Karl's stomach lurched. This time there was no mistaking who it must be. Fear pervaded the room.

Papa rose and gestured to Karl, who, fighting down the terror that rose inside him, led Oma and Rosa into the small study beside the dining-room. His mother went to stand beside Papa and Uncle Rudi. Karl gripped Goldi tightly to him as she gave a low growl.

There was another volley of crashes against the door, and a voice shouted, 'Open up, Jews!'

3

Taken Away

As Papa opened the door, a black-uniformed officer, wearing on his cap the skull badge of the dreaded Nazi SS, pushed past him and strode into the room. Behind him was a local Viennese policeman whom the Mullers had known for years – but now, Karl saw with a shock, wearing a swastika armband.

The officer glared round the room. In the moment of silence, a tiny stifled sob was heard from the study.

'Get the Jewish scum out from there,' the officer ordered the policeman. As Goldi growled, he turned to Karl. 'Shut that animal up, or we'll throw it out of the window.'

Karl rushed to shut Goldi in the kitchen, his body responding without conscious thought. The policeman pushed Rosa and Oma, holding each other, both crying softly, into the room. At the other side of the kitchen door, Goldi whined and scratched.

'Shut up, all of you,' shouted the officer. They gasped as he pulled out a gun. 'We've come for Muller, Jew and Social Democrat supporter.'

Papa stepped forward, his face grey.

'Where are you taking him?' Mama's voice shook.

'For now, to do some street-cleaning,' said the officer, grinning unpleasantly. 'And maybe other things.' He turned to Karl. 'You, fetch toothbrushes. Nothing else.' Did that mean Papa wouldn't be back tonight? No one dared ask.

As Karl re-entered with the toothbrushes, the policeman grabbed Papa and dragged him to the door. Rosa let out a frightened wail.

The officer turned to Uncle Rudi. 'You too!' he barked.

Ignoring him, Rudi bent to comfort Rosa. Without a word, the officer swung round and struck him on the head with his gun. They all heard the sickening crack. Rosa screamed as Rudi fell to his knees, blood trickling down his cheek.

Papa bent to staunch the wound with his handkerchief. The SS officer motioned to them with his gun. 'Get going!'

Rudi struggled to his feet, Papa's blood-soaked handkerchief pressed to his face. From the kitchen, Goldi let out a mournful howl.

At the door, the SS man roared, 'None of the rest you is to leave this apartment!'

For a moment they waited in fearful silence, which was broken only by Rosa's whimpers. Karl could hear them stumbling down the stairs. He hurried to the window. Below, he could see Uncle Rudi, leaning on Papa, struggling along the street, followed by the two Nazis. He watched them until they vanished round the corner.

They tried to fill the endless hours of waiting with little jobs and strained conversation. Mama put out some food, but no one was hungry. Oma sat by the window, peering down at the darkening street. Rosa, refusing to go to bed, fell asleep on Mama's lap.

And then, much later, Oma called from the window, 'Quick, Karl! Here's Papa!'

Through the crack in the curtains, a lone figure could be seen below.

Karl was halfway down the stairs when it struck him. Where was Uncle Rudi?

◆ ❖ ◆

At first Papa could hardly speak. His clothes were torn and splashed with mud and grime, his hands bleeding, his eyes raw and inflamed behind the cracked lenses of his spectacles. He gripped Karl tightly and Karl could smell a sour whiff of sweat and something chemical and pungent.

'Thank God you're back safely,' cried Mama, rushing to the kitchen to heat soup for him.

'Where's Rudi?' asked Oma. 'What happened?'

There was no reply. Karl's heart began to bang uncomfortably.

Then Papa said slowly, 'We had to scrape the anti-Nazi posters off the walls with our fingernails.' He grimaced. 'People were shouting and jeering. Ordinary Austrians like us, families with children.' He blinked his sore eyes. 'Then we were forced to kneel on the pavement and scrub off the slogans, with toothbrushes. For a joke, they said.' Glancing down at his swollen hands, he went on, 'They poured ammonia over us, to burn our skin. All the time the SS, the Hitler Youth, they were screaming at us, shouting filthy things–'

'Were there no police there?' whispered Mama.

'Our own police stood by, even helped them. Then–' His voice broke. Mama held him tight. Finally he continued, 'One of them kicked an old woman who was on her knees beside us, scrubbing. I whispered to Rudi to keep quiet, that it would soon be over. But you know Rudi. He stood up and shouted, "Leave her alone! Is this what you Nazis stand for? Abusing people, kicking old women?" They beat him up–' He swallowed. 'And when I tried to intervene, they kicked me to the ground. Then they dragged him off.'

There was an appalled silence.

'Where did they take him?' Mama asked shakily.

Papa hesitated. 'They said – Dachau.'

Karl paled, recalling the horror stories they had heard about Nazi prison camps.

Oma drew a long, shuddering breath.

'They said it was for a few weeks, so that he would "learn manners",' Papa told her. He added, trying to sound confident, 'I'm sure he'll be back.'

Much later, in bed, thinking about all that had happened that day, Karl felt as if he had suddenly grown older – as if his childhood had flown away from him, leaving a new Karl, harder, angry, expecting the worst.

$\underline{4}$

Swastika

On the tram to school on Monday, it soon became clear to Karl that his city – charming Vienna, with its tall, elegant buildings, its almond trees just coming into blossom – had been transformed by the Anschluss.

Gone were the red-and-white Austrian flags that had been everywhere in the weeks leading up to the expected vote. Instead, almost every building was decorated with black-and-red swastikas and bunting. Huge portraits of Hitler gazed down from hoardings. The old Café Splendide, where Oma used to bring Karl and Rosa for a special treat, had become overnight the CaféBerlin, flying a Nazi flag with a sign: 'Jews not wanted here.'

On the tram, those not in Nazi uniforms had swastika pins or armbands. Youngsters were decked out in blue-and-white Hitler Youth uniforms. Small children carried Nazi flags. Even a little sausage-shaped dog was wearing a jacket with a swastika.

How could things change so quickly? Overnight, Karl had become an outsider in his own city. A cloud of loneliness enveloped him.

A voice said, 'Karl!' He looked up to see Lisl, her long dark hair gathered by a velvet ribbon, taking the seat beside him. But today, instead of their usual easy chat, there was an awkwardness between them.

After a moment Lisl asked, her usually clear voice low, 'Was it a bad weekend?'

'Not good.'

She hesitated. 'I heard hundreds of people were arrested.'

'Uncle Rudi, too.' Karl tried to keep his voice steady. 'And my father had to scrub the streets.'

'I saw some of it,' said Lisl quietly. 'It was horrible.'

As the tram neared Karl's school, she said, 'Those Hitler Youth are everywhere, all of a sudden, with their fancy uniforms. My father wants me to join.' Seeing Karl's expression, she added firmly, 'Don't worry, I told him I wouldn't. These Nazis aren't going to stop us being friends just because you're Jewish.' As Karl rose to get off the tram, she gave him her cheeky grin.

In school, at first, everything appeared reassuringly unchanged. At morning assembly, Herr Klaar, the headmaster, addressed them, his voice low. 'My dear students, these are bad times for the citizens of our country – and I mean *all* citizens, who should be protected by the State. We must pray for our beloved Austria–'

'Ostmark, you mean, Herr Klaar,' bellowed Herr Seiss, the maths teacher, jumping to his feet. 'And surely we should honour our new leader?' Thrusting out his arm, he roared, his eyes on his fellow teachers, 'Heil Hitler!'

Several teachers and students followed suit, some enthusiastically, a few half-heartedly. No one looked at

Karl, or at any of the other Jewish pupils.

On the platform, the headmaster faltered. Then he said, 'I would rather say, "God bless you all".'

◆ ❖ ◆

Summer came, but it was different from any previous summer. To Karl it seemed as though everything was slipping out of its place, going wrong, like music jangling out of tune.

New laws were constantly being announced, laws restricting the lives of Jews, Gypsies, homosexuals, handicapped people – all now to be known as 'non-Aryans'. Karl's parents, along with all other Jews, were notified that their children could only attend Jewish schools. Jews had to sit in the rear sections of trams; they couldn't go into non-Jewish shops, restaurants, sports centres or swimming pools; they had to sell their apartments and businesses to Nazis for next to nothing.

'It's wholesale robbery,' said Papa, his face creased into a worried frown. 'I suppose they'll soon take over the shop. With the anti-Jewish boycott, it's hardly making anything, but it's all we've got.' They had already sold Mama's jewellery and Papa's watch, and the piano that had belonged to Oma and Opa, and they were living on fast-disappearing savings.

Papa had put advertisements in the English papers seeking work as a gardener, a labourer, a domestic – no job was too menial. But there was no response. Every day Papa and Mama set off on a weary round of offices and consulates, to try and get visas so that the family could leave. But virtually no country was interested in letting in penniless Jewish refugees. They returned wearily late in the evening, to eat the meal prepared for them by the children and Oma, who had grown feebler and more fearful since the Anschluss.

And all the time, people were disappearing. At Karl's new school, every morning they checked to see who was missing. The lucky ones, with relatives or friends abroad who could guarantee them jobs, were leaving the country. The others had been arrested, or had gone into hiding.

Austria itself had become a prison camp for Jews. And as the net closed in, increasingly, their 'Aryan' friends abandoned them.

5

Lisl

On a Sunday in late summer, Karl set off on his bike to visit Lisl. Before the Anschluss, they had cycled together every weekend in the Vienna woods, under trees frothing with blossom, or, in winter, wheeling their bikes through thick snow under the stark black boughs.

But since that day just after the Anschluss, when they had met on the tram, he had seen her less and less. She seemed preoccupied, and she was often busy at weekends. It would be good, Karl thought, to talk to her, to be reassured by her friendship and the special feeling there was between them, to laugh as they had always laughed together.

But when he turned down the gravel path leading to Lisl's house, Karl saw with dismay, on a brand-new flagpole beside the magnolia tree, a large swastika flag.

He hesitated. Many people flew the Nazi flag, he told himself; maybe her parents felt they had to. There was no way Lisl could be part of the hateful new Nazi Austria.

As soon as she appeared, however, it was plain to Karl that everything had changed. Holding the door only partly open, clearly trying to keep him out, she told him coldly that Austrians like her were no longer allowed to talk to Jews like him.

Karl couldn't believe what he was hearing. 'But, Lisl, I'm Austrian too!' he cried. 'And you and I are friends—'

'No, Karl,' she said, her eyes fixed on a point over his shoulder. 'Maybe we *were* friends, but we can't be any more. It was all a mistake.' Tossing back her long dark hair, seemingly untouched by his distress, she went on, 'I didn't understand before, but my new leader in the Hitler Youth explained it all to us. Jews are enemies of our country. They're – you're not wanted here.'

Long afterwards, Karl remembered the stony glint in her eyes, the bitter blow of her words, and the turmoil in his mind as he cycled slowly homewards.

◆ ❖ ◆

The summer passed, and autumn leaves snowed thickly onto the grey River Danube. Stalls appeared selling spicy hot sausages and roast chestnuts.

Karl was heartsick. In what he increasingly thought of as 'the old days', the approach of winter had meant ice-skating with Lisl and his other friends, football with Tommy, visits to the cinema. But he never saw his old school friends any more, and cinemas and sports were forbidden to Jews. And since that dreadful visit to her house, he had heard nothing from Lisl.

Once he thought he glimpsed her in the street, in the Hitler Youth uniform she had told him she would never wear. He tried to forget about her, but the memory of her throbbed like a wound.

At home Rosa asked plaintively, 'Why can't we go any-where any more? Why won't Annalise from downstairs play with me? Why is everyone so cross and worried?'

No one answered. Instead, Karl's cousin Tommy brought his little brother Benji, a cheerful toddler, to play with Rosa and keep her amused. Karl and Tommy spent more and more time shut in Karl's room, making model boats and planes together.

One wintry day, when Karl was walking Goldi beside the Danube Canal, an elderly man approached. 'Karl?' he said, 'Karl Muller?'

It was his former headmaster, Herr Klaar, greyer and more stooped than Karl remembered. As they watched the ducks slipping on the ice, Herr Klaar told Karl that he had been dismissed because of his anti-Nazi views; the maths teacher, Herr Seiss, was now headmaster.

He asked about Karl's new school. Then he said sadly, 'I never thought I'd ever have to say this to fellow-Austrians, Karl, but I hope your family are planning to leave the country. It's very bad for Jews.'

Karl, reassured by his concern, asked the question that had been haunting him. 'Herr Klaar, why has it all happened? Why do they suddenly hate the Jews?'

Herr Klaar put his hand on Karl's shoulder. 'It's a kind of madness,' he said quietly. 'For the past few years, things have been very bad in Germany, and here in Austria too. There were no jobs, there was dreadful poverty, money lost its value ... Then Hitler and the Nazis seized power, saying they would put people back to work and make the country strong again.' He sighed. 'But they need a scapegoat, and like all bullies they pick on the weak – people who are in a minority, maybe because they're a different race or religion, or because they have different traditions – and make sure they're blamed for all the country's problems. This deflects any blame from the Nazis themselves.'

It still didn't make sense, thought Karl. It probably never would. But even talking about it with someone who tried to explain sanely and normally, made him feel better, and helped him to block out the things Lisl had said to him.

Herr Klaar turned up his coat collar against the fast-falling snow. 'I must go. It's not safe to be out, for either of us.' He shook Karl's hand. 'Get out, Karl, while you can. It's going to get worse.'

◆ ❖ ◆

And then, one Friday evening, when they had long given up hope of seeing him again, Uncle Rudi came home.

6

The Return

Mama had just lit the Sabbath candles when Rosa, peering down into the street, called, 'Papa! Isn't that Uncle Rudi?'

They all rushed to the window. 'It *is* Rudi,' Papa cried, and hurried downstairs, with Goldi at his heels. 'Thank God,' said Oma, cuddling Rosa, as they waited expectantly.

Goldi loped back in first, her tail waving. But the welcoming smiles froze on their lips. For Papa led in a stranger.

This couldn't be Uncle Rudi, Karl thought – this limping old man, his skin papery, ashy stubble on his face, a filthy cap on his shaved head. One foot was wrapped in a bloodstained cloth, and he gave off a sharp, rank smell.

They stared at him in shock. He put a stick-like arm round Mama. 'I never thought I'd see any of you again.' The hoarseness of his voice couldn't quite hide the rich tones, all that was left of the Rudi they had known.

Oma caressed his sunken cheek. 'My son,' she whispered. 'What have they done to you?'

Rudi looked at her dully. 'You can see, Mutti. They've destroyed me.' He gave a deep jagged cough. 'There was no food, no shelter. My foot was crushed by a rock in the quarries. The things I've seen–'

'Don't try to speak, Rudi.' Gently, Papa led him to the couch and poured him a glass of their precious whisky. 'Drink. Rest.'

'My little Rosa,' said Rudi. 'Where is she?' Rosa stared at him with frightened eyes. He's right, Karl thought painfully, they've destroyed him.

Protectively, they all gathered round as he hugged Rosa. Goldi padded over and settled on his feet with a thump. A faint cackling noise came from Rudi. By the time they realised he was trying to laugh, he had begun to cry.

Later, after Rudi had washed and rested and had his foot bandaged, Rosa and Oma kissed him good night, and the others sat listening as he talked compulsively, puffing constantly on a cigarette. 'They released a few of us, so that our condition would frighten others.' In an instinctive gesture he raised his hand to run it through his once-thick hair, then withdrew it with a grimace. 'They told me that if we don't get out of the country, all the Jews will be rounded up and sent to these prison camps, or worse.'

Papa laughed bitterly. 'As if we aren't trying to leave! We queue for visas every day. No country will take in refugees, especially refugees who have nothing.'

'But we've heard that some young people are being allowed into Britain on special schemes called Kindertransports,' Mama told Rudi. 'They're organised by English Quakers, and other Christians and Jews there. Karl and Rosa would at least be safe. We can all follow them when we get visas.'

Britain! thought Karl, half in longing and half in dread. Far from the SS and the Hitler Youth, the Nazi flags, the jeering, the insults, the violence, the fear – but also far from everybody and everything that was known and dear.

'Believe me,' said Rudi, with chilling emphasis, 'if we are taken to that place I was in, none of us will come out alive.'

7

Kristallnacht

Late on a November afternoon, not long after Uncle Rudi's return, the family heard, from the street, the crash and tinkle of broken glass. Pricking up her ears, Goldi struggled to her feet.

Papa was at the shop. Mama peered cautiously through the window. 'There are crowds,' she said. 'And a light in the sky. Something is on fire.'

'What is it?' asked Oma, her old hooded eyes full of fear. 'Is it the Nazis? Are they coming again to take us?' She twisted her heavy ring with trembling fingers.

'Don't worry, Oma,' said Karl. 'We're safe here.' But were they? The violence they could hear wasn't far away. And what about Papa at the shop?

There was a tap at the door.

'It can't be Papa. He'd use his key,' said Karl.

'Don't open it!' mumbled Rudi, from the sagging armchair by the fire, where he spent most days in his dressing-gown. 'Mustn't let them in. Better to die here–'

'Hush, Rudi.' Mama opened the door a crack. It was their

neighbour, Leni, from downstairs. 'Come in quickly.' Mama locked the door behind her.

'I shouldn't be here,' whispered Leni. 'My husband would kill me if he knew. But I want to tell you to stay inside tonight. They're destroying all the synagogues, the Jewish shops, everything.'

'But why?' cried Oma. 'Why?'

Leni touched Oma's shoulder. 'You've always been good neighbours to me,' she said. 'I don't know why these dreadful things are happening. Apparently a young Jew has assassinated some high-up Nazi officer – in Paris, I think it was. But it's just another excuse. They're all crazy, crazy for blood, and I'm ashamed my husband is among them.' She shook her head. 'I must go back. I just wanted to warn you.'

As she left she said to Mama, 'You should try to get the children out. I wish I could help–'

'Thank you for telling us,' said Mama, her face pale.

Karl began to pull on his shabby tweed coat.

'Where are you going?' said Mama.

'You heard what she said,' said Karl. 'I'm going to warn Papa.'

'No Karli, it's too dangerous out there.'

'I can't just sit and wait here, Mama,' said Karl firmly. 'I must do something, something to help.'

Mama hesitated. Then she wound a scarf round his neck. 'Please, darling Karli, be careful.'

Out in the streets, there was an acrid smell. The sky had an ominous reddish glow. Fighting down rising panic, Karl threaded his way through side streets towards the Jewish area. All around him, shop windows were being kicked in and people were helping themselves to anything they wanted – clothes, furniture, china, bedding, a gramophone. He saw an old woman dragging a pink velvet carpet behind her in the dust.

In Leopoldstrasse, flames were pouring from the synagogue. Uniformed policemen were among the crowd of onlookers. Karl saw the elderly rabbi, coughing and choking in the thick smoke, clutching the holy scrolls of the law and the silver Menorah, the seven-branched candlestick that Karl recognised from the synagogue. Someone grabbed the Menorah from him, and as Karl crossed the road he saw the rabbi sink to the ground, murmuring a prayer. He wanted to stop. But ahead, outside his father's shop, he could see a crowd of Hitler Youth armed with sticks and iron bars.

Propelled by terror, sweat trickling down his forehead, Karl ran. 'Must get to Papa, must get to Papa ...' Like a shadow, he dodged through the crowd. He reached the shop as his father was desperately pulling the metal shutters down over the windows.

Karl rushed to help him, and they got one shutter down. Then the mob was on them, breaking the remaining unprotected window, shouting, swearing, snatching the shoes and boots on display, smashing the glass shelves.

Papa was knocked down, and Karl saw a youth give him a vicious kick with a hobnailed boot. Rage boiled up inside him, dowsing his fear, urging him to hit back. At the last moment sense returned. He couldn't help his father by getting himself beaten up, or worse.

Then, suddenly, they were all gone, on to the next shop, leaving Karl and his father amid the debris.

As he waded through splinters of broken glass to help Papa to his feet, Karl's fog of anger slowly faded. He was left with a mixture of relief and utter weariness, followed by a gathering fear of what might come next.

8

The Merry-go-round

Thinking back, months later, Karl realised that that night – which became known as Kristallnacht, the Night of Broken Glass, because of the smashed windows of thousands of synagogues, shops and businesses – was the beginning of the end for his family, and for all the other Jews. After that night, events moved faster and faster. Karl felt as if he was spinning round on one of the elegant painted horses of the Prater merry-go-round, unable to get off.

The Mullers had to leave their apartment and move into a tiny, cramped flat with Karl's cousin Tommy and his family. Rosa was happy, with Tommy's little brother Benji to look after; but in the unfamiliar surroundings, poor Oma became utterly confused, wandering around at night calling for Opa. She slept only if Rosa lay beside her and Goldi guarded the door.

Sometimes it seemed to Karl that his old, happy, normal life might have been a dream.

And then one day, Mama told Karl that, as a result of the panic after Kristallnacht, extra Kindertransports were being arranged. She had secured places for him and Rosa in a group of two hundred children who would travel to England, leaving in a few weeks.

'We won't tell Rosa until nearer the time. We're trying to arrange for Tommy and Benji to go too,' said Mama. 'It will be so exciting! And you'll be away from all this.' She smiled, too brightly.

Uncle Rudi found an old German-English dictionary he had once used for a play, so that Karl could begin to learn English. It all seemed unreal, until the sight of the strange English words brought home to Karl the huge sea change that was looming ahead.

◆ ❖ ◆

Pre-occupied with all this, Karl noticed one day that spring had arrived, and the chestnut trees in the Stadtpark were in bloom. At the pavement cafés with their gaily-striped umbrellas, people were drinking coffee with cream.

In spite of everything, Karl felt almost happy walking back from school through the sunlit streets. With Uncle Rudi's help, he was learning English. He had tried to put Lisl out of his mind and he was beginning to look forward to the adventure ahead. Mama is right, he thought, it *will* be exciting. Tommy will be with us, and Rosa will have Benji to play with. Surely, he told himself, the rest of the family will get visas soon, and we can all meet in England.

But when he got home he found Rosa weeping, her arms round Goldi, and he saw that Mama's eyes were red.

'What is it?'

'The date of the transport has been changed,' said Mama.

'It leaves tomorrow.'

Karl felt suddenly cold, as if a shadow had passed over him after hot sunlight.

'I don't want to go to England!' cried Rosa. 'Not without Mama and Papa, and Oma and Uncle Rudi. And not without Goldi.' At the sound of her name, Goldi gave Rosa's face an affectionate lick with her sandpaper tongue.

'We need her here to take care of us, darling,' said Mama, her arms around Rosa. 'And we'll all be coming soon.'

'But it's my birthday soon,' murmured Rosa, between sobs. 'I'll be eight. Oma always bakes a special cake, and I promised Benji he could help me blow out the candles–'

'Come,' said Mama, her voice trembling, 'we'll pack your things. Oma will help us.'

'Aren't Tommy and Benji coming too?' asked Karl.

'There's no room in this group, but they'll come in a later one,' said Mama. 'And we'll join you very soon,' she added quickly. 'We'll make a new life – it'll be so much better ...'

She stopped as Papa came into the room. He went to the window and stood with his back to them.

'Papa?' said Karl. He turned, and Karl saw with a shock that tears were streaming down his face.

When Rosa returned, Papa placed his hands on both their foreheads, murmuring a blessing. Then he bent to kiss them.

For a long time afterwards, Karl felt his father's tears damp on his cheeks.

9

Leaving

Karl had left Vienna from the Westbahnhof Station before – carefree departures for family holidays or summer camps. But never like this, late on a dark, windy night, with hundreds of crying children and babies, distressed parents, and Nazi guards coldly looking on.

They had packed hastily. They were only allowed one small suitcase each, and Papa had given Karl his own, covered with bright stickers from past holidays in Austrian lake resorts. There had been no room for their treasures – Rosa's Noah's Ark with its painted wooden animals, Karl's Meccano building set, his collection of comics, his books.

Mama had given them photographs – of herself and Papa, younger and smiling; of the family together in the Stadtpark; of Goldi, tumbling on the grass with Rosa; of Oma in an old-fashioned black dress, her silver hair swept up, a tiny Star of David at her throat.

There had been little time for proper goodbyes, no time even to think.

Tommy had said cheerfully, 'Write and tell me what England's like. I'll see you there soon, and we'll have some fun – they're good at football.' He grinned. 'Maybe we'll even learn to play cricket!'

Oma, the confusion in her mind briefly clearing, went to fetch their grandfather's blue-and-white prayer shawl, in its worn velvet pouch.

'He would want you to have it,' she whispered to Karl. 'Use it whenever you go to the synagogue to pray.' He kissed her cheek; it was sharp and bony, as though all the soft flesh had been eaten away by sorrow.

Then, turning to Rosa, Oma slid the heavy iron wedding ring from her finger and tucked it into her hand. 'To remember us, Opa and me, darling.' She held the child tightly to her.

Rudi gave Karl a small leather-covered autograph book, and gripped his shoulder wordlessly. Rosa cuddled Benji, and stood on tiptoe to give Uncle Rudi a hug. Then she bent and buried her face in Goldi's silky golden coat.

◆ ❖ ◆

Through windswept streets, they walked silently with Mama and Papa. Papa had insisted on coming, despite the danger of being picked up by the SS. 'No one,' he said firmly, 'is going to stop me saying goodbye to my children.'

At the station they joined crowds of parents and children, all clutching their suitcases, as grim-faced Nazi Stormtroopers with guns and truncheons patrolled the platform.

The reality of the separation from his family, and the journey to an unknown world, hit Karl like a sudden blow in the guts as he and Rosa hugged their parents, the comforting arms enfolding them for the last time. They kissed Mama's velvety cheek and Papa's bristly one. Papa dried Rosa's tears with his handkerchief and handed her a new doll and a book about a dog, a golden retriever just like Goldi. Mama, with a forced smile, handed them paper bags with sandwiches and apples for the journey.

Then they had to get into the train.

'Look after Rosa, Karli,' murmured Mama. 'God bless you both.'

'Remember, stay together,' said Papa huskily. 'We'll join you as soon as we can.'

Inside the carriage it was dark. The window-blinds had been drawn by the guards, so that parents and children couldn't see each other.

As his eyes became accustomed to the darkness, Karl saw that the carriage was full of children of all ages. Some were crying; others, the younger ones, not understanding what was going on, were excited at the prospect of an adventure; and two girls of Karl's age were, like him, beyond tears.

Peering through a crack between the blinds, he saw Mama and Papa in the line of quietly weeping parents. His mother, in her best hat, stepped behind Papa to try and hide her tears.

In a kind of daze, Karl stowed the cases in the overhead racks. Thankfully, Rosa had stopped crying and was cuddling the new doll.

A whistle blew. The train hissed, signalling its imminent departure. It shuddered and started to move – slowly, then faster ...

Karl gazed at the rigid figures of his parents, trying to fix their images forever in his mind as they grew smaller and smaller. Then the train, with a shrill whistle, clattered round a bend, and Karl could see them no more.

PART TWO

A Strange Land:
Karl & Rosa: Belfast, 1939

10

Ireland

When the children from the Kindertransport, weary and be-wildered, finally landed at the English port of Harwich, Karl's first thought was: We're free of the Nazis! We can live like human beings again! But the joy and relief that swept through him, trickled away again as he pictured his parents on the platform, and the rest of his family, hundreds of miles away in Vienna.

With Rosa gripping his hand tightly as they crowded off the boat, he told himself that now his most important task was to try to get his family out of Nazi Vienna, to safety.

In the flurry, they only had time to say a brief goodbye to the others who had travelled in their carriage, before they were all split up. The lucky ones had relatives waiting for them; others were going to a reception centre called Dover-court; and some, including Karl and Rosa, were taken to London. There they were met by a pleasant woman, a Mrs Bland, who introduced herself, to their delight, in fluent German. She explained that she was one of the

Kindertransport organisers, and that she was taking them – just for a few days – to her home, where several refugees were already staying.

Thousands of children were arriving on the Kindertransports, she told them, and those who had no family in Britain had to go wherever people had volunteered to care for them. 'Children are being sent all over the country,' she said, 'to foster families, boarding schools, farms, work camps, even castles!'

'Will we be with a family?' asked Karl.

'I'm not sure about that yet,' she replied. 'Anyway, you and Rosa are going to Northern Ireland.'

Seeing Karl's blank expression, she pointed to the place on a map. It looked a long way away. She explained that some Kindertransport children had already been fostered there with local families, while others were being housed in a refugee hostel, which had been set up by the small Jewish community in Belfast.

Northern Ireland? Belfast? A refugee hostel? Karl realised with a jolt that he and Rosa were refugees; they had no home, no country, hardly any money, only a little English. How were they going to manage, alone, separated from everyone they knew and loved, not knowing what might be happening to their family?

He felt tears springing up, and swallowed them down resolutely. It was no use sinking into self-pity. He must stay strong for Rosa, as he had promised his parents.

'Ireland is a beautiful country,' their hostess told them encouragingly. 'And there will be other young people from Germany and Austria. And maybe, in a while, a family will be found to take you in.' She gave them both a hug. 'And while you're here in London, we'll do some sightseeing.'

Karl sent a card home to Vienna, describing Tower Bridge and Big Ben, and the red double-decker buses, and Rosa's amazement at being ushered across a busy road by a policeman, who smiled at her.

◆ ❖ ◆

Nearly a week later, Karl stood on the deck of the Belfast-bound mail-boat and gazed at the rain falling on the dark spread of water. Above his head, gulls shrieked and swooped. Beside him Rosa stood on tiptoe, retching over the wooden rail. How much longer, he wondered, before they finally reached Ireland?

The other passengers were eyeing them curiously, and he realised how different and odd he and Rosa must appear – his brown suit with knee-length trousers, Rosa's button boots and little hat, both of them with labels round their necks giving their names and destination.

Rosa stopped retching and asked for a glass of water. As Karl returned with the water, a man beside them pointed to a shadow in the distance, and said something in English. When he saw Karl did not understand, he said slowly, 'Belfast – Northern Ireland.'

Realising they had almost reached their destination, Karl tried to clean Rosa's grubby face with his handkerchief. Keeping his balance with difficulty on the rolling deck, he went to get their cases.

Then the boat was travelling up a wide expanse of water,

which the man told Karl was Belfast Lough. It was lined with docks and cranes and towering gantries, and in the distance was a forest of tall chimneys, church spires and greenish hills.

Karl had been told to stay on the deck until they were collected. A soft rain was falling. He and Rosa watched people disembark, until it seemed they were the last passengers on the ship. Around them sailors were tying ropes, stacking chairs, cleaning decks.

Still it rained, and still no one came. It seemed hours since they had eaten. Rosa started to cry.

A sailor approached them with two mugs of tea and two sandwiches made with wedges of white English bread. 'You poor kids must be starving,' he said. Seeing they couldn't understand, he showed them with signs that someone was phoning for help.

They gulped down the strong sweet tea, and Rosa was halfway through her sandwich when Karl took a bite and realised with dismay that the tasty pink filling was ham, a forbidden food for Jews. Papa would be horrified. But how could he explain to the sailor?

In the end he extracted the ham from both their sandwiches, to Rosa's resentment. 'It tastes good, and I'm so hungry,' she said plaintively. 'Surely God would understand?'

A voice said, 'Karl and Rosa Muller?' A man in a trilby hat, like Papa's, was beside them, smiling apologetically. 'I'm so sorry, there was a mix-up. The person who was supposed to meet you couldn't come.' To Karl's relief, he spoke German, though with an accent. 'I'm Jack Freeman, head of the Jewish community here in Belfast.' He picked up Rosa's case and shepherded them down the gangway, onto the quay.

As they climbed into his car, parked nearby, Mr Freeman delved into his pocket and gave them each a bar of Cadbury's chocolate, which was new to them. 'Thought you might be hungry.'

Rosa perked up and munched the chocolate. 'Lovely little girl,' Mr Freeman said to Karl. 'It must have been hard for your parents to send you away.'

Karl nodded, not wanting to think about that. He was trying to shake off the dazed, dreamy tiredness that seemed to envelop him, and think about the future, about what this new life was going to be like.

◆ ❖ ◆

Through the car window they could see a low, slate-coloured sky, and small children playing in the narrow streets. Then they turned into a wider street with tall houses and small patches of front garden, sodden in the unceasing rain.

'Are we going to the hostel?' asked Karl, unable to use the word 'refugee'.

'That's right,' Mr Freeman replied. 'It's in Cliftonpark Avenue. They'll have a meal ready for you. It's a bit crowded at the moment – lots of refugees.'

'From Vienna?' asked Karl, hopefully.

'Some of them,' he said. 'And in a few weeks, everyone in the hostel is being moved to a farm in County Down.'

'County Down?' said Karl, taking a bite of chocolate. 'Where's that?'

Mr Freeman smiled. 'Not too far. The farm is about twenty miles from Belfast, on the Ards peninsula, by the sea,' he said. 'It's at a place called Millisle.'

11

Rosa's Doll

On his first few mornings in the hostel, Karl woke at dawn to a rush of homesickness. He had slept in so many different places since he had left Vienna that it took him a few moments, in the mornings, to work out where he was. He lay there, eyes tightly shut, wishing he was back in his own bed in Vienna, with Mama calling him down for hot coffee and fragrant bread rolls. Instead breakfast was a strange bland stuff called porridge, toast, and some new kind of jam called marmalade.

Once he was up, Karl began to feel better. He had made friends with some of the other refugees of his own age – Eva, a graceful girl with gentle brown eyes, who came from Prague, and Danny Grun, from Berlin, who had a thatch of fair hair and an easy, laughing manner and shared Karl's interest in model aeroplanes.

◆ ❖ ◆

A few days after their arrival, Karl and Rosa were called to the chilly downstairs parlour, which smelled of polish. Jack

Freeman was sitting waiting for them, with a strange man and woman. From the kitchen, a whiff of cabbage heralded the evening meal.

'What a sweet little girl!' exclaimed the plump middle-aged woman. 'We'd love to have her.' And she swooped down and gathered Rosa to her. Rosa, her thumb in her mouth, clutched her doll and submitted reluctantly to the embrace.

Karl, trying to concentrate on following the woman's English, saw the kindly balding man nudge his wife and, glancing at Karl, mutter something to her.

Jack Freeman said cheerfully to Karl, in German, 'Well, you kids are both in better shape now than you were the other morning, on the boat!'

The adults had a conversation in fast English, during which the woman cuddled Rosa on her lap. Karl could see Rosa starting to wriggle. He winked at her, shaking his head slightly, and she grew still. Although they didn't know the couple, Karl was aware that it was through the efforts and generosity of all these strangers that he and Rosa and the other refugees were there, and it wouldn't do to be ungrateful.

Jack Freeman turned to Karl and cleared his throat. 'Karl, Mr and Mrs Gould would like to take care of Rosa,' he said in his slow German. 'They don't have any children of their own, and they will give her a very good home in Belfast–'

Mrs Gould put in something in English.

'They would even employ a nanny, just for her,' Mr Freeman translated. 'Unfortunately, they only have room for one child, but they would make sure you saw each other as often as possible.' He paused. 'They will be like parents to her.'

Rosa said quickly, 'I already have parents! My Mama and Papa are in Vienna, and they're coming for us soon.' Mr Freeman translated, and the adults exchanged glances.

'It's very kind of them,' said Karl, 'but my parents said we should stay together.'

Mr Freeman nodded sympathetically. 'I understand. But I think it would be best for Rosa. She'll have everything she could want. I believe your parents would agree. Other refugees have been fostered by families here, and they're happy. I'm only sorry that there aren't enough families for all of you.' He lowered his voice. 'Conditions on the farm where you'll be going will be hard, at first. You'll be sleeping in tents. And Rosa has been sick ...'

As if to reinforce his words, Rosa coughed. Mrs Gould produced a tiny lace-edged handkerchief. Rosa took it politely, slipped down off her lap and went to Karl.

He put his arm around her. Soon after their arrival in Belfast, she had fallen ill with a chest infection that still lingered. And although, during the day, she seemed happy with the other children, on several nights she had been found sleepwalking. Perhaps living in comfort with Mr and Mrs Gould would be better for her than the farm.

Quietly Karl explained to her what was being suggested. 'Would you like to go with them?' he asked her. 'You'd have lovely toys and a nice room.'

Rosa considered. 'Have they got a dog like Goldi?'

Karl grinned wryly as Mr Freeman translated for the Goulds. After a moment, Mr Gould said, 'I think there's a puppy next door that she could play with.' He smiled at Rosa and produced a big white box, tied with coloured ribbon, which he held out to her. She took it shyly.

Inside was an enormous china doll, with wiry yellow hair and a pink-and-white checked dress. Rosa gazed at it, torn between the gleaming doll in the box and the battered, grimy one she was holding.

Mrs Gould leaned over and put the new doll in Rosa's arms, tucking the old one away in the box.

'Now,' she said firmly, 'I think that's settled.'

They all rose, Karl with an uneasy feeling in the pit of his stomach. The decision seemed to be out of his hands. Was it the right thing? How could he be sure what was best for Rosa?

Jack Freeman patted his arm reassuringly. 'It will be all right, you'll see,' he said cheerfully. 'Rosa will be very happy.' He turned to her. 'You go with your new auntie and uncle. Just think, you'll have another car ride!'

Rosa hesitated. 'I have to pack my case.'

Mr Gould said something in a hearty tone. 'There's no need,' Mr Freeman explained to her. 'You'll have all new things! Aren't you a lucky girl?'

Karl hugged Rosa tightly, murmuring, 'I'll keep all your things safely, with the photos and Oma's ring. You can see them whenever you come.' Then he gave her a little push towards the Goulds, who were waiting at the door. Their smiles reminded him of his own mother's too-bright smile when she told him about the Kindertransport. If he felt like this now, how must she have felt, sending both him and Rosa into the unknown?

'I'll see you soon, love,' he said to Rosa. 'Don't worry; these people are kind.'

Surely they will be? he thought, watching anxiously through the window as Rosa climbed into the Goulds' small black Morris Minor.

Karl sighed and turned his thoughts to the farm to which the refugees would soon be moving. Millisle – that was it. He didn't even know how to spell it, never mind what awaited him there.

12

Another Journey

Yet another railway station, thought Karl, though this time in Belfast, a long way from the Westbahnhof in Vienna.

Once again clutching their suitcases, the refugees were shepherded onto the train by a tall, commanding man in boots and riding jodhpurs. His German had a strange accent. Karl's new friend Danny whispered that the man was Anton Senesh, the Millisle farm manager, himself a refugee from Hungary. He had visited the hostel before Karl's arrival.

'He doesn't smile much,' Danny told Karl.

'I've heard he speaks five languages!' said Eva.

'All of them very loudly,' added Danny.

Eva, sitting opposite Danny and Karl, had one of the younger girls on her knee. Karl had noticed that she hid her homesickness by mothering the younger children. He wished Rosa was there to be mothered.

The train let out a mournful whistle and set off amid clouds of steam. Through the grimy windows they glimpsed rows of small red brick terraced houses, some of their gable ends elaborately painted with murals. Karl noticed one of a man on a white horse, with slogans and the figures '1690'. Mr Senesh told them that the decorations were for the July holiday, and that most of the people who lived there worked in the big Harland and Wolff shipyard, whose giant cranes and gantries they could see nearby.

Once they had left Belfast behind, grassy meadows, cultivated fields and hedgerows strewn with wildflowers and a blaze of red poppies, slid past the window. Eva pointed to huge pale sheets lying over some of the fields, rippling in the wind as though they were floating on a green sea.

'D'you think they blew off someone's washing-line?' she asked.

'It'd have to be some giant's washing,' grinned Danny. A woman in the carriage, seeing their puzzlement, told them with Mr Senesh interpreting – that it was linen cloth, woven from flax plants and spread out to be bleached white in the sun and air.

'If you come back next spring,' she told them, 'the flax fields will be a mass of blue flowers.'

A memory darted into Karl's mind, of himself and Sasha, wading through drifts of bluebells in the Vienna woods in springtime, and bringing back a bunch for Mama. Mama would love the flax flowers. Perhaps next spring she and Papa would be here to see them ... He remembered what Oma used to say, when anyone wished hard for something, 'From your mouth to God's ears.' But Karl sometimes wondered, on the dark days, whether God was listening.

◆ ❖ ◆

At the busy seaside town of Donaghadee, they were met by a tubby little man with a shock of white hair and a sweet smile, who greeted them in what Karl joyfully recognised as Viennese-accented German, and helped to load their luggage onto the Millisle bus. He told them to call him Yakobi, and explained that he would be responsible for their health and welfare on the farm. 'They chose me because I'm from a medical family,' he said, adding, with an ironic shrug, 'But my only skill is playing the saxophone!'

'I myself have a degree in agriculture,' boomed Mr Senesh from the seat behind, 'but I've never actually managed a farm before.'

'What can we do? We're refugees,' responded Yakobi. Smiling around at the group, he caught Karl's eye. 'All of us, we just have to do our best.'

As they drove through the town, Yakobi pointed out the shops and arcades and amusements, and the Regal Cinema, which lifted Karl's spirits. Perhaps he could go to the pictures again – maybe see Judy Garland, or a Western like the ones he used to see with his friends, before the Anschluss.

The bus chugged along narrow country lanes, winding through little rounded green hills. Eva exclaimed at the foamy meadowsweet in the hedgerows, whose scent wafted in through the windows of the bus, and the delicate scarlet and purple flowers that Yakobi told them grew wild here, and were called 'fuschia'.

Mr Senesh became quite chatty. He explained that the farm they were going to had been long disused, but that the Belfast Jewish community had leased it to house the refugees. A group of older refugees was there already, and they would all be joined by a few families, and two or three local farm workers who were helping them get the farm going.

Karl tried to push down the familiar jittery feeling. Now, alone, without even Rosa, he would have to get used to yet another new home. A farm, he thought. What do I know about Irish farms?

13

The Farm

Karl never forgot that first night at Millisle. Climbing down from the bus, they smelled the salty tang of the sea and heard waves breaking on the other side of a low wall. A misty, penetrating rain fell, seeping through their clothes. Carrying their meagre luggage, they followed the short, square figure of Yakobi up a narrow lane and into a muddy cobbled farmyard.

The new arrivals gazed dispiritedly at the crumbling, musty stables, the empty barns, the dilapidated stone farmhouse, the muddy fields full of long grass and thistles and giant dandelions, all under the heavy, grey cloak of the sky.

After their supper – surprisingly good vegetable soup with sandwiches, eaten in an old stable with rain trickling in – Mr Senesh stood up.

'Don't worry,' he told the subdued group. 'We're going to work very hard – all of us, even you children. We'll build dormitories and recreation rooms, and the Belfast community is getting us a new water pump so that we can have hot showers. We'll clear the fields and plant them. With everyone's help, we will create a good, productive farm.' Cheered by this, they all applauded.

Later, after they had negotiated the outside privies – smelly, muddy holes in the ground, with raised wooden planks across them – they tried to settle down in their sleeping bags in two large tents beside the farmhouse.

With the wind howling outside and raindrops pattering steadily on the canvas, Karl drifted off into confused dreams. His parents were being arrested by the SS; a tearful Rosa was begging Karl to find her lost doll; the boat on which they were travelling to Belfast began to fill with water, which rose and rose until it was up to their waists ...

He woke to screams and shouts, to find his pyjamas and sleeping bag soaked and the groundsheet a morass of mud. Yakobi and Mr Senesh appeared, the leaking tents were dismantled, and they all spent the rest of the night shivering on benches in the farmhouse, sipping hastily made hot Ovaltine drinks.

'It's great, this outdoor life,' Danny muttered to Karl. 'And instant cold showers, too.'

Karl sighed. 'It can only get better,' he said.

◆ ❖ ◆

And, indeed, it did get better. The next day dawned fresh and mild. Birds sang in the apple orchard, and the sky, newly rinsed by the previous night's rainstorm, was a soft blue, with a scattering of fleecy clouds.

After breakfast they were given boots and work clothes, and the younger ones waded through the fields, picking up stones and uprooting weeds and chopping down spiny, purple thistles, while the older ones dug, hoed and planted. A newly whitewashed cowshed provided a dry place to sleep that night.

Days passed, and then weeks and months. The pangs of homesickness, the sense of loss that lay like a stone in his heart, never entirely left Karl, but they softened into a familiar dull ache. Gradually a routine was built up. And, despite stings, bites, blisters, and sore muscles from the unaccustomed work, he began to feel that at last some order had been put into his chaotic life.

And bit by bit, on what they all came to call 'the Farm', they built new wooden dormitory huts, a cow byre, workshops and storerooms. A barn was transformed into a dining-hall; living quarters were provided for the adults, and soon there were cart-horses, cows, two dogs – dearly loved by the children – hundreds of chickens, and even a farm cat.

Two local farm workers – craggy, weather-beaten men of few words, but with a store of farming knowledge and wisdom – patiently taught the refugees to plough and harrow and thresh. With their help, the ground was cleared, dug and planted; potatoes and vegetables grew; and by that autumn, acres of tall, golden wheat and barley swayed and rippled in the fields.

◆ ❖ ◆

All through that first year at Millisle, Karl was busy and occupied, learning English, settling in at the local school, attending night courses in Donaghadee, getting a sense of the place and the people. But the urgent need to get his family to safety was always burning in his mind.

At first he got letters from home, their hopeful tone clearly trying to hide the worsening situation, telling him that they hoped Tommy and Benji would soon be on a Kindertransport to England. Karl wrote back cheerfully, saying that he was fine and that Rosa was happy with the Goulds – although, on her last visit to the Farm, she had clung to Karl when it was time to leave, whispering in German, 'Why are Mama and Papa taking so long? They said, that night at the railway station, that they'd come for us soon.'

On one of Mr Freeman's visits to the farm, Karl spoke to him about finding jobs for his parents so that they could get visas to leave Vienna – although he knew how much the Committee had already done for them all, raising funds to support every Kindertransport child brought to Ireland.

'It's very difficult, Karl,' said Jack Freeman sadly. 'There are so many people trying to get out. Even if we could find jobs for them, the Nazis often demand large sums of money to give them visas. Still, I'll put them on the list. And you could write to the Refugee Committee in London, and to any relations you have outside Austria, to see if they can do anything.'

Karl thanked him. But the only relative he knew of was a distant cousin in America, with whom his parents had tried, and failed, to make contact before the Anschluss; and he didn't even have her address.

14

The War Comes

And then came the news: Nazi troops had marched into Poland. On a sunlit September day, everyone gathered in the Farm kitchen to hear the weary voice of Mr Chamberlain, the British Prime Minister, announcing on the radio, 'Britain is now at war with Germany.'

Karl recalled what his father had said on the day the Nazis had marched into Vienna – that Hitler would try to swallow up all the countries of Europe. Karl's sense of relief that at last someone was going to fight Hitler and the Nazis, clashed with his fear for his family and all the remaining Jews now trapped.

And the news grew worse. In the first year of the war, country after country in Europe fell to the victorious Nazis. In June, even France was defeated, leaving only Britain and Ireland free, surrounded by a Nazi iron ring.

After that, there was no way of knowing what was happening to Karl's family. Occasional brief Red Cross messages just told him that they were well and still in Vienna. He had no idea whether Tommy and Benji had made it onto one of the Kindertransports, which had ceased as soon as the war began.

Karl knew that everyone on the Farm had similar worries about families they had been forced to leave behind, and similar desperate hopes that they would somehow be reunited.

◆ ❖ ◆

On a breezy day in that first summer of the war, Karl toiled up the hill behind Millisle village to the Ballycopeland windmill, long ago used for grinding grain. In the year he had been at the Farm, the mill had become his favourite place – a quiet spot where he could be alone and just sit and think.

Although the door was nailed up, he had found a narrow gap he could just squeeze through to get in. Climbing up the rickety wooden ladder inside the stone walls, he glimpsed the huge sails of the mill, now stilled. Below him, long-tailed swallows swooped in graceful arcs, in and out of their nests under the eaves of the miller's house.

Beyond the gently rounded countryside of Ards lay the dark waters of the Atlantic, where Karl knew enemy U-boats were prowling like hungry wolves, searching for ships to attack. It was hard to believe that only the strip of the Irish Sea, and Britain itself, lay between the Nazi threat and the peace of the Farm.

Karl tried to switch his mind to more cheerful topics. Soon he was going to visit Rosa at the Goulds' house. And some of the boys from Millisle village, whom the refugees had got to know at the local school, had challenged them to a football match.

And Mr Senesh had announced that a group of young volunteers from Dublin was coming to work on the Farm for the summer. Perhaps that would mean trouble. Karl knew that some of the refugees might resent people from the neutral South.

What would they be like? he wondered idly, as he set off back down the hill to the Farm – these people from a country not involved in the war, living normal lives, as he once had.

PART THREE

The Farm: Judy, Karl & Peewee: Dublin & Millisle, Summer 1940

15

The Bombshell

In their small, cramped house in Dublin's Portobello, not far from the Grand Canal, Judy Simons was having an argument with her parents – not an unusual situation, for her. She had been busily cutting out photos of her favourite film stars from *Picturegoer* magazine when her parents dropped the bombshell about a farm in Northern Ireland, and how nice it would be for Judy to go there for a few weeks to help.

'Me? A farm?' said Judy incredulously. 'I can't even tell a weed from a flower. Why should I spend the summer slaving on some farm, miles from anywhere?'

'On this farm, there are young refugees from Europe,' said her da quietly. 'They're Jews like us, and they escaped from the Nazis just before the war–'

'But we're not even in the war, here in Dublin, so what've refugees in the North got to do with me?' protested Judy. 'They probably don't even speak English.'

Da, his expression worried, as it always was these days, looked at her sorrowfully. In the corner of the room, the whirr of the sewing-machine suddenly ceased as Judy's mother lifted her foot from the pedal. She was running up a pink taffeta frock for Judy's elder sister, Tilly, to wear at the hop, the weekly dance at the Jewish Youth Club. Why bother, Judy thought, when Tilly probably wouldn't be going?

Judy knew everyone considered seventeen-year-old Tilly – three years Judy's senior – to be clever, kind and good, the opposite, in fact, of Judy. The opposite in appearance, too, thought Judy, who longed to be frail and slender and delicate like Tilly, instead of disgustingly healthy – chubby, as her older brother Michael put it when he wanted to annoy her – and sulky-looking, with thick brown hair in two boring plaits.

And in fact Tilly was the cause of all the trouble, the reason why Judy was being made to go to this remote alien place – Millisle Farm. By rights Judy should have been going on the usual family holiday to the seaside in Bray, staying in Stein's Kosher Hotel or in one of the white-painted guest houses which lined the promenade. Everyone would be there, having ice-cream and fizzy drinks on the beach, riding on the Ghost Train, and spending rainy afternoons in the amusement arcade or in the cosy warmth of the Royal Cinema.

Of course Judy had to admit that Tilly's illness was hardly her fault. It had started with a persistent little cough, for which the doctor had prescribed Famel's cough syrup. Gradually Tilly had grown paler and thinner, with a hectic flush on each cheek like a spot of rouge. Then one night, in the small bedroom the girls shared – neat as a new pin on

Tilly's side, a mess on Judy's – Tilly had coughed and coughed; and afterwards Judy, shocked, had seen vivid red splotches on the white handkerchief Tilly held to her mouth.

◆ ❖ ◆

'It must be TB,' Judy's friend Nora from next door said, when Judy told her. 'Consumption, my granny calls it. My auntie had it. My da said it's a serious illness. Tilly'll have to go to a sanatorium and sleep out in the open. My auntie said she nearly froze to death.' She added quickly, 'Still, she's a bit better now.'

But then the doctor said that Tilly need not go to the sanatorium for the present, as long as she rested in bed and got lots of fresh air. So it was decided that instead of going to Bray, the family would stay for a while in a remote cottage on the windswept Hill of Howth, and Judy would spend the summer away from home on Millisle Farm. The Dublin Jewish community had been asked to aid the refugees by sending a group of volunteers up to the North to help on the farm – in the kitchen, the laundry, and, Judy thought sullenly, heaven knew what else.

Judy had begged her parents to at least let her go on holiday with Nora and her family to Bundoran, where Judy was sure she would have a good time. But from her da's frown and her ma's sighs, she could tell there wasn't a chance. She knew they thought she would run wild with Nora in Bundoran, and that she would be better supervised on the farm – definitely not a point in its favour, as far as Judy was concerned.

'The refugee farm will be a new experience for you, dear,' said Ma encouragingly. 'And you'll meet people your own age who've had to cope with terrible experiences.'

Then Da said gently that going to Millisle would be a good deed. 'The Jewish communities in Belfast and Dublin are contributing to the farm,' he said, 'and so are the Churches, and the Refugee Committee in London.' He sighed and went on, 'But there are thousands of these child refugees all over Britain. They came with nothing, and if the farm can be made to pay, it will support them and provide training for their future.' He patted her cheek. 'Judy, dear, we may not be in the war here, but this way you can help people who are suffering. And it's only for a few weeks.'

'But Northern Ireland is in the war,' protested Judy. 'It might be dangerous.'

Da shook his head. 'All the papers say it's much too far for the Nazi planes.'

'And anyway, they wouldn't risk bringing the neutral South into the war,' added Michael.

Nobody mentioned Tilly's illness as one of the reasons for Judy's being sent to Millisle until Michael, who liked to remind everyone he was a medical student, said the next morning, in that showing-off way Judy found so annoying, 'TB can be infectious. It's risky for someone your age to be in contact, especially as you've been sharing a room.' Peering into the spotted bathroom mirror and slathering his hair with greasy Brylcreem, he added, 'I'm going to be gone anyway, working in hospital. And it's safest for you to be right out of the way.'

So that was that. The only bright spot was that volunteers

working on the farm got two shillings and sixpence a week, plus their keep; it was the first money Judy would ever have earned. And a sympathetic Nora promised to write and tell her all about Bundoran.

And so – after affectionate farewells from her parents, a mocking grin from Michael, and irritating tears and kisses blown across the room from Tilly – Judy found herself on the Great Northern train to Belfast, and to her first taste of a farm, of Northern Ireland, and of the war.

16

Over the Border

In Dublin, the war had made only a few changes to everyday life. People complained about the shortages of tea and tobacco, and about the glimmer man, who went around on an orange bike, testing the hobs of cookers to see if rationed gas was being used outside the regulation hours. The shortage of fuel brought out bikes and horse-drawn carts and even canal boats. Trains, running on wood and turf, were slow, and sometimes the passengers had to get out and gather wood for the boiler. But apart from a few inconveniences, life on the whole remained much the same as before.

So when, on a damp July day, the group from Dublin arrived at Belfast's Grand Central Station, they were stunned by the echoing, noisy building thronged with sailors and airmen, civilians and police, and soldiers in khaki uniforms, laden with rifles and backpacks.

A war poster read, 'Careless Talk Costs Lives'. Careless talk is probably what I do all the time, thought Judy. How could it do anyone any harm? One of their group, Norman

Isaacs, who had relations in Belfast and liked giving out information, told them it was a warning that enemy spies might listen to what you said and pass it on to the Germans and help them win the war. Everyone thought that sounded far-fetched.

Then someone pointed towards another poster, 'Dig for Victory!', showing an enormous boot driving a spade into the clay. 'I suppose we'll be doing that on the farm.'

'Well, *I'm* just going to help with the baby animals,' stated Judy firmly.

'Surely we'll have to do what we're told?' murmured Pearl, the only other girl in the group.

Judy wished Nora, or anyone with a bit of spirit, was with her instead of Pearl. Just my luck, she thought, to find myself in a war zone with drips like know-all Norman, with his horrible hairy brown jacket with those bulging pockets, and Pearl, who blushes when anyone talks to her – plus a crowd of refugees.

◆ ❖ ◆

Two people from the Farm were waiting at the station.

'You are all welcome,' said the white-haired older man. 'My name is Yakobi.'

On the bus, he pounced on a wine gum Norman offered him. 'Here, we need sweet coupons for this, because there is sugar rationing,' he explained. 'And I have a very sweet tooth, so thank you!' He gave a twinkly smile. 'But, as they say, there is a war on, so we must not complain.'

The younger man was introduced as Gaby. He wore a

small skullcap on his dark hair, and he reminded Judy of one of the handsome film stars whose photos adorned her bedroom wall at home. But when she asked pleasantly if he was a refugee, he nodded grimly and stared out of the bus window. Very friendly, Judy thought resentfully. I suppose they'll all be like that.

The Belfast streets were crowded with uniformed soldiers, troop carriers, and menacing armoured cars. Windows were criss-crossed with strips of sticky paper; according to Norman, this was to prevent flying glass if there was an explosion. In the bus there were notices about registering for clothing-coupons and ration books, and warnings about carrying gas masks, observing the blackout, and taking shelter when there was an air-raid warning. Judy wondered uneasily what an air-raid warning sounded like.

'This war stuff's a bit scary,' whispered Pearl, her eyes following Judy's. Judy shrugged, unwilling to admit – especially to Pearl – that she was scared too. Yakobi smiled reassuringly at both of them.

When they arrived at the Farm, they picked their way, laden with luggage, across the yard, between huge smelly 'cowclaps', as Yakobi called them, and a few stray chickens.

Judy and Pearl were led into an empty dormitory which had rows of iron beds and bunks, with white gas-mask containers slung over them. On a table there was a pile of comics and magazines in English and German, among them *War Weekly*, *Beano* and *Hotspur*. Yakobi indicated two narrow beds, each with a tiny metal cupboard beside it – much too small, Judy noticed, for all her stuff – and left to take the others to the boys' dormitories.

Outside they could hear voices with foreign accents, and someone laughing. Judy sank onto the hard, narrow bed and thought, What on earth am I doing in this strange place?

17

Enemy Aliens

Early on the morning of the Dubliners' arrival, Karl was working with Danny and a few others in an immense field half a mile from the Farm, spread with cut swathes of grass.

'I wonder what they'll be like,' said Danny. He and Karl had become good friends over the past year. Danny's way of seeing the lighter side of things reminded Karl of Rudi – the old Rudi, before the Anschluss.

Karl stopped forking the hay into haycocks and stretched his aching shoulders. 'Who?' he asked, squinting over towards the distant farm buildings to see if there was any sign of the cart bringing refreshments.

'This new crowd from Dublin, of course,' said Danny, giving Karl a mock dig with his rake. 'Two of them are girls – or "young ladies", as Mr Senesh put it.'

He was interrupted by a shout which echoed down the hayfield, 'Breakfast!'

The figures dotted round the field flung down their rakes and pitchforks and headed for the shade of a towering sycamore tree at the edge of the field. The group, all in drab work clothes and rubber boots, and ranging in age from eight to eighteen, clustered around Yakobi like chicks around a mother hen. He handed out milk bottles full of hot sweet tea, and thick slices of wheaten bread spread with yellow farm butter.

Karl leaned back on the grass, gulping his tea gratefully, and gazed up into the delicate green canopy of the branches, speckled with sunlight. Above the soft cooing of the wood pigeons, the chatter of the others eddied around him. They mostly spoke English nowadays, though in the months after their arrival they had used a mixture of German and English as they battled to learn the strange new language.

◆ ❖ ◆

'What about a game of ping-pong tonight?' Danny was asking Susi Linden, whose fine curls were stuck to her forehead with sweat. He gave her his most winning smile; but then, encountering the disapproving gaze of her older sister Rina, he retreated, with an elaborate bow in Rina's direction.

Susi seemed disappointed. All the girls liked Danny and his jokes – all except sharp-tongued Rina, peering at him through her little round spectacles. She was overprotective, as most of the refugees were of their younger brothers and sisters.

But although Rina often appeared cross and cranky, Karl knew differently. Once, passing the small cubicle where she lay sick with an infection, he had overheard her hopeless, desperate weeping. It wasn't an unusual sound at the farm.

He had hesitated and then moved on. What comfort could you give, when you yourself suffered the same bitter pangs of anxiety and homesickness? Mostly, people tried to hide their feelings, or dealt with them in whatever way they could.

Karl kept his emotions locked inside. Outwardly cheerful, he depended on the friendship of Danny and Eva, and a few of the others. But something held him back from getting too involved with anyone. Deep down, he carried painful memories. Lisl still appeared in his dreams, turning on him cold-eyed, as she had done the last time he saw her.

People were starting to plod back to the hay-field. Karl picked up the rake with calloused hands and set to work.

◆ ❖ ◆

Three hours later, the sad plaint of a distant Angelus bell sounded noon. This was the signal for the workers to return to the Farm for showers, lunch and the radio news. Itching all over from the hay that got inside their clothes, they piled wearily onto the cart, which an unsmiling Gaby had driven over from the Farm.

'Maybe this new crowd will help with the hay,' said Karl.

'And the chickens, and the potatoes, and the harvest,' added Danny. They had lapsed into German, as they sometimes did when they were together.

'They'll be useless,' said Rina sourly. 'They're city people; they'll know nothing about farm work—'

'But we knew nothing when we came,' argued Karl. 'They'll learn, like we did.'

'Well, I went with Yakobi to collect them today at the station,' grunted Gaby, 'and they're a pretty stupid bunch. One of them asked me if I was a refugee! So stupid – as if it wasn't obvious. And they're probably no use at football either.'

'The South of Ireland, where they come from, isn't even in the war,' said Rina. 'They call it "The Emergency" there. So how can they understand about refugees like us? Even here in the North, we're all called "enemy aliens", just because we're Austrian and German, even though everyone knows the Nazis are the enemy, not us.'

Turning the cart out on to the lane, Gaby said, 'Some people think we're spies. When the war started, in Britain they just rounded up everyone from Germany and Austria, refugees along with everyone else.'

The cart slowed to allow six or seven cows to make their ponderous way towards the byre to be milked. Gaby went on, his expression dark, 'Every one of us over sixteen would be rotting in internment camps on the Isle of Man right now, if Mr Senesh hadn't persuaded the tribunal in Newtownards that we weren't any risk to Northern Ireland.'

'But still, we're so restricted!' Rina protested. 'We have to be in by ten. We can't even travel the few miles to Belfast without a police permit ... It's ridiculous! How could we be spies, after everything the Nazis have done to us–' She broke off, near tears. Susi glanced at her anxiously.

They finished the journey in silence, but as they got down from the cart, Karl said to Rina, 'You know, these new people from Dublin volunteered to come. They may not be bad.'

Rina shrugged, unconvinced, and went off with Susi in tow.

Karl, though he was interested in the strangers, had more pressing problems to worry about. According to Mrs Gould, Rosa was still sleepwalking. That must mean she was unhappy. And last week the Refugee Committee in London had replied to his letter about his family; they had explained how difficult it had become, since the war had started, to help people trapped inside Nazi Europe, and had enclosed a list of other refugee aid organisations to write to. Trying to keep his hopes up, Karl had written yet more letters.

Luckily, he had other, lighter things to concentrate on – like the line-up of the Farm football team for the match against the village side. Apart from Gaby, none of them were very talented, and they were still three players short, *and* there was no coach.

At the dormitory, Karl snatched a towel and made for the showers. Sooner or later, no doubt, despite Rina's and Gaby's unwelcoming comments about them, he'd get to know the newcomers.

18

Chickens

The morning after the Dubliners' arrival, Judy was the last to appear in the farmyard, where everyone, including Norman and Pearl, had assembled for their work assignments. So far, she reflected gloomily, as the steady drizzle seeped through her clothes, nothing had gone right.

The previous night, she had tossed on the thin mattress for what seemed like hours, trying to get to sleep. The wooden walls creaked; there were coughs and murmurs, sobs from a little girl in one of the bunks, then whispering as the soft-spoken girl who had shyly introduced herself as Eva went to comfort the crying child. If this goes on, Judy had thought, I'm never going to get a wink of sleep.

In the morning, she had overslept; and as she bolted her breakfast, a girl with glasses had come over and accused her of taking other people's rations. Apparently the little jars and dishes of butter and sugar, jam and cheese – all with labels which Judy hadn't bothered to read – were people's weekly rations, and you were only supposed to use your own.

'How was I to know they were rations?' Judy had said in an injured tone.

The girl had sniffed. 'Do you not even say sorry?' She had gone back to her friends, obviously complaining to them in German about Judy.

◆ ❖ ◆

In the yard everyone clustered around a board, on which there were lists of names in spiralling foreign handwriting.

'I can't make head or tail of these peculiar names,' complained Judy.

Norman fished in one of his jacket pockets and produced a magnifying glass. 'I'm a Boy Scout,' he said smugly. 'Always prepared.' It was no help.

Eventually Mr Senesh, the farm manager, appeared and sent each person off to a job. Norman went off to the hayfield, and Pearl to the laundry. Judy was quite pleased to be sent to the hen-house, where she expected a pleasant, peaceful morning cuddling fluffy baby chicks.

When she arrived at the low wooden structure, she was greeted by a fresh-faced girl not much older than Judy herself, with a mop of dazzling red hair.

'I'm Grace Doherty, and I'm from County Tyrone. I'm in charge of poultry,' she said briskly. 'Here, put these on – you don't want to ruin your clothes.' She handed Judy a pair of boots and some baggy overalls, and took her into the hen house.

Inside it was hot and dark, and there was such a disgusting smell that Judy was sure she would throw up. She had to clear out the filthy straw, covered with hens' droppings, and put in fresh straw. After that, she was just going off for a rest when Grace called her back.

'You haven't finished yet,' she said sweetly. 'You have to collect the eggs and pack them, and help me mix the mash and feed the hens.'

Collecting the eggs didn't sound too bad. Judy, already taking off her work clothes, figured it would only take a moment. But it turned out there were what seemed to be hundreds of eggs all over the place, hidden under straw and in the yard, with dirt and bits of straw stuck to them. She had to wash them, dry them and pack them into cartons in dozens, with chickens clucking hysterically all round her.

'Oh no!' exploded Judy, as she broke an egg down her good cable-knit sweater. 'It looks as if someone's been sick on it.'

'Don't worry,' Grace told her kindly. 'Everyone breaks eggs at first. Just keep in mind that they're rationed.'

By the time she had finished, Judy's boots and clothes were covered in muck and chicken mess, and she felt more like strangling the chicks than cuddling them.

Back in the dormitory before lunch, Pearl said, 'Your sweater's an awful mess.'

'You don't say,' snapped Judy. 'And if I have twenty showers, I'll never get rid of this awful smell.'

Eva, who had appeared with Pearl, put in apologetically, 'I am afraid the showers are not working. I heard there is something wrong with the new electric pump.'

'Thanks a lot!' Judy peered into a little cracked mirror and let out a shriek. 'My face! It's so rough and blotchy! And I left my hair loose this morning because I'm sick of the plaits, and now it's like barbed wire. And,' she moaned, flinging herself on the bed, 'I'm wrecked, and it's only lunchtime!'

◆ ❖ ◆

After supper that night, the Dublin group hesitantly followed the others to the recreation room – known as the rec – where people were playing ping-pong, cards or billiards, chatting, or listening to the radio.

They stood together awkwardly, watching some younger boys huddled over a game of monopoly. Norman pointed out to Judy the strange names on the board – Graz and Wien, instead of O'Connell Street and Kimmage. One of the players, a boy with a mischievous grin, explained in quite good English that he'd brought the game with him from Austria.

'I never realised they do the same sort of things we do,' Pearl whispered to Judy, 'like playing table-tennis and monopoly.'

'And I've heard they go to the cinema in Donaghadee on Saturdays!' said Norman, overhearing. 'The refugees get in for free! Maybe it won't be so bad here.'

Judy gazed out of the window at a field where a few boys were kicking a football. 'I think it's pretty awful here. They're all so mean and unfriendly.'

'Shhh,' said Pearl, glancing around anxiously. 'They might hear you.'

'Who cares?' Judy snorted.

At nine o'clock, everything stopped for the news. Just like

at home, thought Judy, who had always found the war news boring. But here everyone, even the younger ones, listened intently to the details of the Nazi invasion of the Channel Islands. Afterwards there was a buzz of anxious talk around the war map of Europe, on the wall, which had boundaries and armies marked on it with coloured stickers.

'It's funny,' said Pearl. 'Nothing's happened here so far, but the war seems much more real than at home.'

Gaby, on his way out, overheard her. He stopped. 'Of course, it must be very nice for you at home in Dublin.' There was an edge to his voice. 'Plenty of everything, as you are not in the war.'

'There isn't plenty of everything,' said Norman indignantly. 'There are shortages – petrol, cigarettes–'

'No cigarettes? How terrible,' muttered Rina, looking up from the gramophone records. 'Maybe you don't know this, but we have lost more than just cigarettes.'

There was a tense silence. Then Yakobi, who had come in to play billiards with Danny and was listening quietly, touched Gaby's shoulder. 'Gaby, Rina,' he said softly. 'These people have come to help us on the Farm. We should thank them, not criticise their country. And anyway, I believe many people from the South have volunteered with the British forces to fight against the Nazis.'

Rina's lips thinned. 'Maybe,' she said. 'But I do not understand how any country can be neutral against evil people like the Nazis.'

The others glanced at each other as Rina and Gaby banged out of the room.

'I am sorry,' Danny said quickly. 'To us the war is so

important ...' Turning to Norman, he tried to defuse the tension. 'How about a game of ping-pong?'

They all watched Norman and Danny play, each being over-polite to the other. Danny played with easy grace, while Norman lumbered about, sweating in his heavy jacket – he seemed to wear it day and night, thought Judy. At the end of the game, it was obvious that Danny had let Norman win.

Back in the dormitory, Judy muttered to Pearl, 'These refugees hate us. I wish we could get out of here. Maybe we could run away.'

Pearl was struggling into her woollen pyjamas. 'It's not that bad,' she murmured. 'That blond one, Danny, is quite nice.' She blushed. 'And he did say he was sorry.'

19

Rescue!

A few days later, Karl sat alone on the low sea wall near the Farm, overlooking the dunes, a series of sandy hillocks with tufts of coarse grass and bracken – a favourite playground for the children. The tide was going out, and in the shallows, a heron stood motionless, its neck coiled, its long thin beak pointing sharply, waiting for unwary fish.

Nearby, beside a rock pool fed by trickling rivulets, two little girls huddled with shrimping-nets. Karl's thoughts jumped to Rosa, whom he had visited in Belfast the previous week. At the Goulds' house, in a leafy avenue, Rosa had hugged him tightly and led him by the hand to her room. It was a dream nursery, with a little white bed, shelves of clothes and toys, a painted wooden rocking-horse, teddy bears and dolls. A white-aproned nanny was ironing a pile of frilly dresses.

'She doesn't seem to like the new doll we gave her,' Mrs Gould had said, as they sat downstairs drinking what Karl called 'Irish tea' – strong and brown, with milk and sugar, quite unlike the weak tea with lemon he had drunk in Vienna. She went on, 'That scruffy old doll is falling apart, but Rosa keeps asking for it. And we have such lovely books and annuals for her, to help her to learn English, but the only book she wants is the one in German that she brought from home!' She pointed to the book, thumbed and worn from use. 'Is it true that it's about your family's dog?'

'Not exactly,' said Karl. 'But at home in Vienna we have a dog like this.'

'And who's Benji?' added Mrs Gould. 'She keeps asking when he can come to play.'

As Karl kissed her goodbye, Rosa had whispered tearfully, 'Karli, Auntie says I walk in my sleep. But in the morning I don't remember.'

Overhearing, Mrs Gould had said heartily, 'Now then, Rosa, we do sleepwalk sometimes, but we're getting better.' She smiled at her. 'Most of the time, we're a very happy little girl, aren't we?'

After that visit, Karl had been left with a sense of unease about Rosa. Maybe he and Rosa staying together, as their parents had told them to, mattered more than toys and pretty dresses. Thinking about it now, Karl decided he would discuss the matter with Yakobi, who always had time to listen to people's troubles.

The broad stones of the sea wall felt warm to his skin. Listening to the squealing gulls and the soft inrush of the waves, Karl rolled up the sleeves of his faded check shirt – donated, like many of the refugees' clothes. He tilted his head back, relishing the weak beams of a shy, unaccustomed sun.

Roused by a shout and the thunder of hoofs, Karl swung his legs over the wall. A girl in mud-stained dungarees was running down the lane towards him, screaming hysterically. Behind her stumbled a cow, letting out loud groans of pain. And behind the cow was a young boy in a cap, flourishing a stick and yelling something that Karl, accustomed as he thought he was to Ulster speech, could not make out.

As the strange procession drew nearer, he could distinguish the girl's shouts, 'Help! It's a bull!'

Karl jumped down. To stop her cannoning into the wall, he held his arms wide. The girl, one of her plaits unravelled, tears of fright streaming down her cheeks, ran right into them. For a second he held her gingerly. The stink of manure wafted from her clothes. Then he stepped round her, so that he was between her and the terrified animal, which he recognised as Alice, one of the Millisle cows. The cow stopped dead.

'It is not a bull–' he started to say; but the girl broke in furiously. 'Of course it's a bull! It's got horns, and that bellowing–'

Karl managed not to smile. 'All cows have those little horns. They are usually taken off when they are young.'

The girl glared at him. He went on soothingly, 'Her name is Alice. She has been sick. That is why she is upset. And she wants to be milked.' He indicated the cow's heavy udders, full of milk. 'She won't hurt you.' He was about to add, 'Wait till you see a real bull!' but he stopped himself.

The cow regarded them fearfully with rolling eyes, its wide nostrils flecked with foam.

Karl recognised the girl, still panting, as one of the new-comers from Dublin. Gazing at her, he recalled a discussion among the refugees about the new arrivals.

'They're such twits,' someone had said. 'They don't even care about the war.'

'And one girl's really spoilt,' Rina had said. 'That one with plaits. She's always complaining. And taking everyone's rations.'

◆ ❖ ◆

The boy with the stick had reached the cow, and stood stroking its damp, quivering side. He was small, with sandy hair; he was wearing a torn shirt and short trousers, and his boots were almost knee-deep in muck.

'What happened?' asked Karl.

Judy spoke first. 'Someone told me to go and help bring the cows to the byre for milking,' she said fiercely, trying to re-braid her hair. 'I went into the field with a stick and shouted at this bull, or cow, or whatever it is. Then it bellowed and ran at me. I fell into a cowclap–' She stopped and peered down at her dungarees, screwing up her face. 'Ugh! That stuff stinks!'

'That's the best of cow dung,' protested the boy. Seeing her disgusted expression, he explained, 'It's good manure.'

'What's good about it?' she snapped.

'It's the stuff that makes wee flowers grow.' He spoke slowly to her, in his sweet piping voice, as though talking to a small child. Turning to Karl, he went on, 'Mr Teevan, the vet on the Ballywalter Road, sent me to fetch Alice. He needs to treat her udder. It's all warty–'

'Oh, *please* ...' Judy looked as though she was going to throw up.

'D'you work for Mr Teevan, then?' asked Karl.

'I'm just helping him out.'

'I don't think I've seen you around before,' said Karl.

'I'm not long here,' said the boy. 'I'm from Belfast.' Noticing Judy's tear-stained face, as she leaned against the wall shakily trying to fasten her other plait, he plucked a sheaf of rough grass from beside the road and tried to wipe the dirt off her dungarees. Karl picked another handful and followed suit. The cow bent her head, tore out a clump of grass, and slowly and deliberately began to munch.

'Sorry you got a fright,' the boy said to Judy, as they brushed ineffectually at her clothes.

She scowled. 'Stupid cow.'

'I know you're from Dublin,' said Karl. 'I've seen you in the rec. You are Judy, I think?'

'Judy Simons,' she said shortly.

'I am Karl Muller.' There was a pause.

'I'm Peewee Crawford,' the other boy put in helpfully, springing up onto the wall.

'*Peewee?*' repeated Judy.

'It's the name of a wee bird,' he said, blushing a little. 'My granny says when I whistle, or play the flute, it sounds sweet, like a peewee bird.' He grinned, showing uneven teeth. 'Anyway, it's better than Nathaniel. That's my real name.'

'Yes,' agreed Karl, laughing. 'Peewee is better.' There was something engaging about this cheery boy with the ready grin. Karl went on, 'Do you play your flute in an orchestra?'

'A band,' said Peewee. 'We play in the march on the Twelfth, but it's cancelled this year because of the war.'

'What is that – the Twelfth?' asked Karl.

'D'you not know about the Twelfth?' Peewee seemed amazed at his ignorance. 'It's a parade, and a big meeting in a field,' he explained. 'A grand day out, on the twelfth of July. To remember King Billy and 1690.'

'Ah,' said Karl, recalling the pictures on the gables of the terraced houses in Belfast. 'The man on the white horse.'

'Aye,' said Peewee. 'That's right. King Billy, and the Battle of the Boyne. I'll tell you the story some time.'

'It must be nice to play music,' said Karl. 'At home I tried out for the Vienna Boys' Choir, but my voice wasn't good enough.'

Judy and Peewee looked blank. 'A boys' choir?' asked Peewee.

Karl could not understand anyone not knowing about the Vienna Boys' Choir. 'It is famous,' he told them. 'They sing all over the world.'

'Do they now?' said Peewee. Then, jerking his head towards the Farm, he said to Karl, 'You're one of that foreign crowd, aren't you?'

Karl nodded. 'I am from Vienna.'

After a moment Peewee asked hesitantly, 'D'you mind me asking, what church do you all go to?' He went on quickly, 'It's just that our neighbour next door told my granny that the foreign crowd at the Farm didn't go to church at all!'

'We have our own synagogue, on the Farm,' answered Karl. Seeing Peewee's baffled look, he explained, 'It's a kind of church.'

'There's lots of churches here,' said Peewee, 'but I never heard of one of those – at least, not in the Shankill, where I come from.'

As Karl opened his mouth to explain, the cow lifted her head from the grassy verge and gave a low moan.

'I'd better go,' said Peewee. He glanced at Karl. 'I could come up to the Farm one night and teach you to play the flute, if you like. D'you know the song, "The Auld Orange Flute"?'

Karl shook his head. Peewee began to whistle with piercing sweetness.

'Do you mind?' said Judy. 'I've got a headache from that cow roaring.' Karl saw that her tears had dried into grimy tracks on her cheeks.

As he slid down off the wall, Peewee gazed at Judy curiously. 'I never met anyone from Dublin.'

'And I never met anyone from this Shankill place,' she said. 'Are you an evacuee?'

'Kind of. My uncle's away in the navy, on the convoys, so we're here to look after the pub till the war's over.'

'Is the pub in the village?' asked Karl. He had never set foot in a pub, though he had noticed several in Millisle's main street.

'Aye,' replied Peewee. 'Crawford's.'

Judy interrupted. 'Listen, I'm going to get these clothes

off, before I stink everyone out of the place. See you.' And she stumbled off, in her oversized rubber boots.

Karl and Peewee followed her slowly back up the lane, the cow ambling in front of them.

'That girl, Judy – is she ...' Peewee stopped.

'What?' asked Karl, a defensive note in his voice.

'If she's from Dublin, like, I was wondering if she was a–' He hesitated. 'A Roman Catholic.'

'Ah – no,' said Karl cautiously. 'She's Jewish, same as most of us refugees on the Farm. That's why we have a synagogue.'

'So you're–'

'Yes,' said Karl patiently. 'I'm a Jew too.'

There was a puzzled silence. Then Peewee said, 'Well, are you Protestant Jews, or Roman Catholic Jews?'

Karl shook his head. 'We're just Jews.' Peewee nodded uncertainly.

Karl smiled to himself. This was a long way from Nazi Vienna, he thought, where the fact of being 'just Jews' could mean the difference between life and death.

Karl turned down the path that led to the Farm and Peewee raised his stick in farewell.

Then Karl stopped. 'Peewee,' he called back to him. 'Do you play football?'

Peewee's face lit up. 'Do I ever!' he grinned. 'My brother Wee Billy and me, we're champions!'

He added, 'At least, that's what our granny thinks.'

20

Homesickness

On Fridays, work finished early at Millisle, because of the Sabbath. As everyone hurried back from the fields, the laundry, the dairy and the workshop, there was a rush for the showers, and the echoing dormitory filled with chatter and laughter.

Putting on her best dress – wine-red, with a little white collar and two pockets, run up by her ma – Judy complained to Pearl, 'I can't get this dirt out from under my fingernails. And my back's killing me.'

'I know,' said Pearl. 'It's from bending double in the potato field.'

Eva, pulling on a pretty embroidered blouse, which Judy reckoned she must have brought from home, said sympathetically, 'We were all aching like this at the beginning. It will get easier.'

'I don't see why we should do that kind of work,' said Judy. 'I'm going to tell Mr Senesh.'

'Oh, you'd better not do that,' said Pearl timidly. 'He might be angry.'

Judy, irritated, continued brushing her hair over one eye, in a style that she hoped made her look like a film star. That morning she had received a letter from Nora describing all the fun she was having in Bundoran – bathing, going to hops, staying up late. It sounded great, thought Judy, a whole lot better than Millisle and mean refugees and drippy Pearl. Judy had also had a letter from home, mainly about Tilly, who was being very brave, and, though still weak, was allowed to get up for a while each day. And of course, her mother had added – rather as an afterthought – that they all missed Judy.

Judy felt a twinge of resentment at the way everything at home seemed to revolve round Tilly, and a pang of home-sickness at the thought of them all preparing for the Sabbath – the delicious smell of chicken noodle soup from the kitchen; Tilly setting out the tall brass candlesticks that their grandmother had brought with her, years before, from her native Poland; Da pouring out the sweet red wine and reciting the blessing over the two twisty loaves of white bread ...

And here she was, stuck in this strange place, with these difficult people. She had had yet another clash with Rina, this time in the dairy. Judy, grumbling loudly that turning the handle of the wooden churn made her arms ache, hadn't noticed the bell ringing to signal that the butter was ready. Only Rina's intervention had stopped it from being ruined.

'You'd get things done quicker if you stopped complaining all the time,' Rina had snapped, scooping out the butter and pouring a can of fresh milk into the churn. She had pranced off before Judy could respond.

In fact, the only bright spot here, Judy reflected, was that boy Karl, who had rescued her from what she would always think of as the bull. At least he hadn't spread the humiliating story, for which Judy was grateful. Last night in the rec, she had told Pearl a censored version, in which she remained totally dignified, and manure wasn't mentioned.

'Is Karl the boy who's usually with Danny?' Pearl had enquired, gazing around.

'Yes, but he's not here now,' said Judy, who had already scanned the room for him. 'He's quiet and thin, with a sort of wing of brown hair over his forehead and greeny-grey eyes. He smiles in a sad kind of way, and he's very polite.'

Pearl had said, 'You must have got a really good look at him.'

◆ ❖ ◆

As usual on Fridays, everyone was spruced up and in good humour as they piled into the converted barn that served as a dining-hall, and sat down at the long trestle tables. There was a babble of noisy talk in a mix of accented English, German and other languages unknown to Judy.

A slim auburn-haired woman, her husband and two little girls beside her, stood to light the Sabbath candles.

'They are Mr and Mrs Franck. They help with running the Farm. They are from Prague, like me,' Eva whispered to Judy and Pearl. She added, in a tone of longing, 'Their family is all together.'

Mr Senesh recited the Hebrew blessing, and cups of wine were passed round for everyone to take a sip. Then there was a song to welcome the Sabbath. Most people sang, but a few sat silently, and a sad little boy Judy had noticed before – usually clinging to Yakobi – started to cry. As Yakobi went to him, she said to Eva, 'That little boy must be sick. He seems to cry a lot.'

Eva, who always appeared so serene, glanced at her, and Judy was startled to see tears in her eyes too. Eva said in a rush, 'Yes, of course he is sick – sick for his home and his parents, like all of us. The Sabbath song reminds him.'

From across the table, Rina threw Judy an accusing look.

Pearl had also overheard. 'Surely you could guess why he's crying?' she said to Judy, unusually sharply. For once, Judy had no reply.

Eva blew her nose and smoothed her hair; tonight, Judy had noticed with grudging admiration, it was gathered in a single honey-coloured plait in which gold strands glinted. After a moment, Eva picked up her knife and fork.

'Sorry,' said Judy. It was not a word she used often.

21

Dancing the Hora

As they gathered in the rec after supper, Judy spotted Karl and pointed him out to Pearl. Karl caught her eye and smiled over at them. He wasn't exactly a film-star type like Gaby, thought Judy – Gaby, who seemed to be with a different girl each time she saw him. But it was fair to say that, in a clean white shirt with his hair slicked down, Karl didn't look at all bad.

Rina, perhaps making the effort because Yakobi was there, grudgingly threw out a general invitation to a game of ping-pong. Judy refused sharply. But she was somewhat taken aback when Norman and Pearl accepted and made up a doubles game with Eva. And Karl seemed to have disappeared. Judy, feeling left out, sorted listlessly through the gramophone records – mostly classical, with a few swing and jazz, and none of them of any interest to her.

After a while, Karl reappeared with Danny. Judy brightened up and grinned a greeting. But, to her disappointment, they merely gave her a polite nod and headed over to the table, where they immediately became absorbed in some kind of model plane they were making.

Bored, Judy flicked through *Picturegoer*, the film magazine she had brought from home, glancing enviously at the photos of the beautiful, glamorous star of the new Hollywood romantic film, *Gone With the Wind*, at its opening in London.

She couldn't avoid hearing the persistent clatter of the ping-pong ball, punctuated by frequent apologies from Pearl.

Whatever about the others, Judy told herself, I still hate it here.

◆ ❖ ◆

But later just as Judy was contemplating going off to bed in a huff – everything, surprisingly, livened up. Some of the older ones came in, and suddenly they were all dancing in a big circle, with their arms round each other's shoulders – dancing the Hora, a traditional dance that Judy knew from the Jewish Club in Dublin. The refugees started it, and eventually everyone got pulled in. They danced faster and faster, on and on, till the room melted into a blur. Almost everyone was laughing hysterically. Judy saw Karl whirl past, then Yakobi, then Danny, beside Susi, her little curls flopping prettily on her forehead. Even Rina was dancing. Gaby, dark and serious as always, stamped out the steps almost in a frenzy.

After the dance finally ended, the room and the people seemed to Judy to carry on swirling around. At midnight, still dizzy, they tottered across the cobbles, past the looming farm buildings. Above, a half-moon shed a fitful light over the blacked-out farm.

'That girl with the little curls, Susi, is really pretty,' murmured Pearl. 'Danny was looking at her in the dancing.' She went on, with her usual blush, 'He's awfully nice, isn't he?'

'Yes, but Susi's big sister Rina thinks Susi is too young to have a boyfriend – even if it's Danny,' said Eva with a laugh. 'And everyone's a bit afraid of Rina.'

Judy nearly said, 'That's because she's so snappy and superior,' but she decided maybe she'd better not upset anyone yet again. Instead, she remarked casually, 'Danny's very friendly with that other boy, Karl.' Even in the dark, she was aware of Pearl's sideways glance.

'Poor Karl,' said Eva. 'He is worried about his little sister, Rosa. He'd like her to be here.'

Judy wanted to hear more about Karl and his sister, and about Eva and the others. All the refugees, she reflected, seemed to be bonded together in an enclosed group, shutting other people out.

But tonight, in the warmth and excitement of dancing the Hora, the invisible curtain between the two groups had, if only for a few brief moments, been plucked aside.

22

The Letter

The stables were Karl's favourite place on the farm. Sometimes Gaby was there, quietly grooming the horses with surprising gentleness. But today, there was no one. The two hefty Clydesdale horses, Molly and Jean, peered out over the half-doors, hoping for carrots or a sheaf of juicy grass. Karl stroked their silky muzzles and ears, and they gazed at him with their gentle eyes and made soft whickering sounds.

Inside there was a warm, horsy, leathery smell. Heavy saddles and bridles and grooming-brushes hung on nails. In the shafts of sunlight, tiny motes of dust spun.

Sitting on a heap of straw, Karl opened his letter. After breakfast every day, an elderly refugee, who lived at the end of the Farm lane with his family, delivered the post. Balding and chatty, and known, ironically, as the Postilion – the German word for postman – he had an annoying habit of telling everyone what was in their letters as he gave them out. The refugees grabbed the letters hungrily, and then disappeared to read them in private.

This was the first time since the war had begun that Karl had received a proper letter from his parents, rather than brief messages. Cautiously worded, it had been smuggled out, and judging by the multiple stamps and postmarks it had travelled a roundabout route.

His mother began with anxious enquiries about Karl and Rosa, and continued, *Since the war began, there are no visas for Britain or Ireland. We're still enquiring about other places, but it's very difficult. Conditions here aren't good. We've sold almost everything to buy food. Leni has helped us, although it's dangerous for her.*

Many people have to leave for the east. Karl knew this meant they were being deported, maybe to prison camps. *Tommy sends love. Although he didn't catch your train, he and Benji may get another one.*

Karl puzzled over this. Since the beginning of the war, there had been no more Kindertransports. What was the 'other train'?

He read on. *Oma has become very confused. She talks as though your dear Opa were still alive, and your Papa and Uncle Rudi were little boys again.*

Every day the Nazis announce new rules to make us into 'unter-menschen', sub-humans. So I'm afraid there is sad news about our beautiful Goldi. Last month, all pets belonging to Jews were taken away and destroyed.

Karl gasped, overcome by a wave of despair, pity for Goldi, and anger. How could he ever tell Rosa?

But there was worse. At the end of the letter, his father had added a few lines in a hasty scrawl.

Karl, you must say the Kaddish, the prayer of mourning, for your poor Uncle Rudi. He took his life while his mind was disturbed and in despair. It was instant; he didn't suffer. We are all terribly sad. It's fortunate that poor Oma doesn't really understand. Thank God you and Rosa are out of all this horror, in a place of safety. Be strong.

Your loving Papa.

PS Don't tell Rosa these things. She is too young.

Sobs shook Karl's body. He remembered a feeble, trembling Uncle Rudi pressing the autograph book into his hand in a mute farewell, as they left for the station. He tried to hold him in his mind as he had been before the Anschluss – handsome, vigorous Uncle Rudi, clowning about, teasing Papa, pretending to toss Rosa up in the air. Karl recalled him saying, when there had been talk of having to leave Austria, 'How could I earn a living in another country? Whoever heard of an actor who can't speak the language?' He had grinned. 'I'm not much good at mime!'

For some time Karl crouched in the corner of the stable, his head buried in his arms, fighting the welter of helplessness and misery. He tried to pray, but his words seemed empty and meaningless.

Something soft tickled his bare arm. He opened his eyes to see the workhorse's huge, feathery white feet beside him. Jean gave him a gentle nudge, and he smelled her sweet oat-scented breath and felt her solid warmth.

Comforted a little, he tried to take heart. He must keep it all inside him, stay strong for Rosa's sake, be cheerful all through her visit to the Farm next Sunday, and redouble his efforts to get the rest of their family out of that hell.

As for himself, as soon as he was old enough he would join

the ATC, the Air Training Corps, in Donaghadee, as many of the older refugees had. He would train for the Air Force, or the Pioneer Corps, so that he could join the fight against the Nazis.

He decided to go for a walk, to calm himself down. And after supper he would help Danny with the model Spitfire. He had found that concentrating on a careful and intricate task, like the balsa-wood plane, helped stop despair invading his mind. Maybe later he would play a game of ping-pong with that girl, Judy, from Dublin. She had been so angry when the cow had chased her; but she had stood for a strange moment in his arms – though she had smelled to high heaven!

Karl dried his face with his handkerchief, patted Jean's shaggy neck, and left the stable.

◆ ❖ ◆

As he set off towards the Ballycopeland windmill, a shout made him turn. Danny and Eva caught up with him.

'Where were you?' asked Danny impatiently. 'We were looking everywhere.'

'Just taking a walk,' said Karl casually, hoping the traces of tears didn't show.

'Did you get a letter?' asked Eva. 'The Postilion said he thought you got bad news.' It was uncanny how he always knew what was in the letters, thought Karl.

'My uncle died,' he told them shortly. No one was startled by this kind of news. They probably thought Rudi had been shot, or deported, or died in prison; things like that had happened often enough, even before they had left Austria. Karl didn't feel ready to tell them the truth. What did it matter? In a sense, the real Uncle Rudi *had* died in Dachau.

Danny and Eva waited in sympathetic silence. Without knowing the details, they understood how he felt, and that he didn't want to talk about it.

Danny flung an arm around him. 'Don't forget football practice tomorrow,' he said. 'Though our playing seems to be getting worse, not better. Anyway, I've asked that Dublin fellow, Norman, to join the team. He's not bad. A bit of a know-all, though.'

Karl struggled to switch his mind to football. 'I forgot to tell you, Danny, I've got us another player. He's small and fast, and really keen. He might be good on the wing. He's coming along to the next practice.'

'*Wunderbar*!' shouted Danny. 'Who is he?'

'His name's Peewee.'

'His name's *what*?'

23

Remembering

Some of the refugees resented the regular visits from the Belfast Refugee Committee members and their families. 'We're on show again, like animals in a zoo,' Rina complained, as they watched cars chugging into the yard on the following Sunday.

Karl darted over to open a car door, and helped out a little girl holding a very big doll.

'It's his sister, Rosa,' Eva told Judy, as they watched from the window of the rec. 'She is always dressed like a princess!' Rosa's hair was in sausage-shaped ringlets, and she wore a frilly dress with a pink sash, white ankle socks, and black patent-leather ankle-strap shoes. Within seconds she had stepped straight into a cowclap, to the concern of the couple getting out of the car, and the amusement of everyone else.

While the Goulds conversed with Mr Senesh, Karl led Rosa to the rec.

'Rosa, this is Judy, from Dublin,' said Karl. Rosa looked

up at her from under her lashes. 'She is shy,' Karl told Judy, 'but her English is quite good.'

He seems so proud of her, thought Judy, more like a father than a brother. She couldn't imagine her own brother ever fussing over her like that.

'Rosa wants to see some of the photos we brought from home,' Karl told them. He turned to Judy. 'Maybe you would like to come?'

Judy was surprised by the pleasure she felt. Karl was always kind and polite to everyone, but Judy had rather expected that, after the bull episode, he would show some special interest in her. At last he had, though it was a strange invitation.

'Yes,' she said.

◆ ❖ ◆

Karl wasn't sure what made him invite Judy that afternoon. Perhaps he hoped her presence might make looking at the photos with Rosa easier, less emotional. Or was it that Judy's manner, sharp and spirited, reminded him of Lisl?

Not wanting to think about Lisl, he grabbed Rosa's hand and set off, with Judy hurrying behind. They stopped for a moment for Rosa to stroke Tabby, the Farm cat; then they crossed the yard to the empty cow byre, which smelled pungently of animals. They went up a ramp and through the workshop, where Karl told Rosa he was learning to help with Farm repairs.

'But surely you don't keep these photos in the workshop?' asked Judy.

'My new shoes are dirty,' said Rosa plaintively. 'And this dolly is heavy.'

To distract her, Judy asked, 'What's her name?'

'My real doll from home is called Mitzi. She's being washed,' said Rosa. 'This one isn't called anything.'

Karl pushed open a heavy door and led them into a musty room, piled high with battered suitcases covered with stickers and labels.

'These are the cases we brought on the Kindertransport,' said Karl quietly to Judy. 'Only one each.' She stared, unaccountably shocked at the sight.

Rosa went straight to a suitcase at the bottom of a heap, and Karl knelt down to open it, with Rosa squatting beside him. With the air of a magician, he pulled out a pair of short leather trousers and a green felt hat with a jaunty feather stuck in the band. They giggled as Karl plonked the hat on his head with a grimace.

'Our best clothes! Not quite right for here.' He added, 'Of course, our parents didn't know we were coming to a farm.'

He rummaged through the case, and as he drew out an envelope, something metallic tinkled to the floor. Judy stooped to pick it up. It was a ring, crudely made of a heavy, dull metal.

'What's this?' she asked.

Karl said nothing. After a moment, Rosa said, 'It's Oma's wedding ring. The iron ring. She gave it to me when—' She stopped.

Karl quickly put the ring back in the case. Sitting on the dusty floor, he took the photos out of the envelope.

'That's my Mama and Papa and Uncle Rudi,' said Rosa, pointing excitedly. 'And that's me with Goldi!'

Judy looked at the unshadowed, smiling faces in the photographs. 'Is this your grandma?' she asked.

'Yes, our Oma,' said Karl, 'at my bar mitzvah, on my thirteenth birthday.'

'Look, Karl,' said Rosa, 'here's one of you with Lisl.'

'Give that to me,' Karl snapped, snatching it out of her hand. Judy and Rosa stared at him.

So he's not always so polite and perfect, thought Judy. Intrigued, she asked, 'Who's Lisl?'

'Just someone I knew,' he said shortly.

'Cooee, Rosa!' came a voice from outside. 'It's time to go, dear.'

Karl turned urgently to Rosa. 'Are you happy with the Goulds, Rosa?' he asked. 'Yakobi says that, if you want to, maybe we could ask for you to stay here on the Farm.'

'Uncle and Auntie are nice to me,' she said slowly. 'Today we're having pink blancmange for tea. And for my birthday, we're going to Duffy's Circus.' Then her face clouded and she added in a rush, 'But at night they lock my door in case I sleepwalk, and hurt myself. Anyway Karli, when Mama and Papa come to the Farm for us, I must be here, mustn't I? And Goldi might be with them, and Benji–'

Judy and Karl exchanged glances. Taking Rosa's hand, Karl said, 'I'll talk to them. You'll come soon.' He didn't have the heart to tell her that, judging by the replies from some of the organisations he had written to, they would have a long wait before their parents came for them. Still, there were more replies to come; and Mr Senesh had written as well. There was no point in discouraging Rosa, destroying her hopes.

As they stood waving off the Goulds' car, Judy said to Karl, 'Rosa's sweet. And thanks for letting me see your photos.'

There was an awkward pause. Careful not to mention Lisl again, she added hesitantly, 'You must miss your family.'

Karl nodded wordlessly.

24

Saving the Hay

Early the next morning, word came from Mr Senesh that everyone should report at once to the hayfield, where the race to save the hay was under way.

Karl, helping to load the dried haycocks on to the cart, heard, in the distance, a mournful cuckoo call. As he worked, his mind shot back to the photo of Lisl, which had so disturbed him the previous day.

Where had it come from? Karl had been unable to tell his parents about Lisl's rejection. His mother must have put in the photo, mistakenly thinking Lisl was someone he would want to remember. And, as a result, he had let down his guard for a moment – in front of Judy, too.

Afterwards he had torn up the photo and decided to try and avoid Judy. Some part of him feared revealing to her that old Karl, open, optimistic, vulnerable.

Hearing his name called, he straightened up, and his heart gave a great leap. Peewee was approaching along the ditch, and bounding behind him was – surely it was Goldi?

Karl dropped his pitchfork and ran to meet them, for a second seeing nothing but the intelligent brown eyes, the gleaming creamy-gold coat, the tail waving like a banner. Then Peewee whistled, and the dog turned back to follow at his heels. Karl's heart slowed and he drew a shuddering breath.

'Hey, Karl!' said Peewee. 'Mr Teevan, the vet, is down with Molly; she's going to foal.' Karl could only nod. Following his gaze, Peewee said, 'Fine wee dog, isn't he? He's a retriever. We call him Carlo.'

'Yes,' said Karl quietly. 'He is – a fine dog.'

'You look flat out. I'll give you a hand.' Seizing the pitchfork, Peewee glanced up at the threatening sky, where folds of bruised, dark cloud were building up. 'We better hurry, wee lad. It looks like rain.'

◆ ❖ ◆

High in the elm trees, clouds of rooks wheeled and called, as the last load of hay was brought in that evening. Despite the fine drizzle, the smaller children sat excitedly high up on top of the creaking Farm cart. The hungry, weary haymakers, waving away clouds of midges, followed slowly on foot.

Back at the barn, Mr Senesh, in a yellowing panama hat, directed the storage of the hay. The kitchen had been busy all day with preparations for a special supper for the farm residents and neighbours, to thank them for their help with the haymaking.

When everyone gathered in the dining-hall, there was a

moment's quiet for the blessing, then a burst of noise and laughter and a clatter of cutlery as they all fell on the food.

Karl ate hungrily, forcing himself to blot out the disturbing image of Goldi, which Peewee's dog had conjured up earlier. The good-humoured, unthreatening presence of Peewee, sitting beside him in a too-large shirt borrowed from Karl, soothed him. Peewee had appeared at the Farm a few times since their first memorable meeting, helping with the work, giving Karl flute lessons, joining in football practices. He had become quite at home among the refugees, perhaps because he too was a stranger in Millisle. Despite – or perhaps because of – their totally dissimilar backgrounds, Karl found he could ask Peewee about aspects of his new life in Northern Ireland which still puzzled him – the different religions, customs and traditions rooted in a complicated history.

Appreciatively, Peewee swallowed the last spoonful of soup. 'That was good.'

'Any news about the foal?' Danny asked him.

Peewee shook his head. 'Mr Teevan said it could be hours yet.'

'I hope everything will be all right for Molly,' said Susi anxiously.

'Don't you worry about Molly,' said Peewee. 'She's strong as – well, as a horse.' He grinned, shovelling in a baked potato. 'Where's Judy?'

'It's her and Pearl's turn for the kitchen,' said Eva. They could see Judy, not looking too pleased, carrying heaps of dirty plates.

Peewee turned to Karl. 'I told my ma about you,' he said,

'and you having to leave all your folks behind because of the war. She said yourself and Judy should come and have a real Ulster tea with us.'

'I don't think I have had this kind of tea,' said Karl.

'You'd meet my brother, Wee Billy,' said Peewee. He added, with pride, 'He's in the Young Soldiers Battalion of the Inniskilling Fusiliers.'

'Your brother is a soldier?' asked Karl, impressed. 'I would like to talk to him.'

'He might be home on leave when you come.' Peewee paused. 'He often goes to see his girlfriend, Eileen, in Belfast, but she's sick at the minute.' Attacking a wedge of apple tart smothered in custard, he added, 'So will you come for tea?'

'I would like to. I'll ask Judy also,' said Karl. 'But, you know, there are some things we're not allowed to eat.'

'Like what?'

'Pork and shellfish,' said Karl. 'Ham, bacon–'

'You mean you can't have rashers?' said Peewee incredulously. 'You poor wee craturs.'

Karl smiled wryly. He had never seen that as the worst of his problems.

◆ ❖ ◆

Anton Senesh rose to his feet, his strong voice stilling the hubbub. 'I want to thank you, neighbours, friends, helpers, for your hard work.' He paused. 'We know the war news is not good. In the skies over Britain, air battles are beginning. Mr Churchill, the Prime Minister, calls it the Battle of Britain –

the gallant few against the evil might of the Nazi Reich. We pray for these brave men, and for all those in the war.'

Gazing round the dining-hall, he went on, 'But here in Millisle there is good news. Thank God, with your help, the hay has been saved to feed our animals through the winter.' He smiled. 'And a foal has been born to Molly.'

25

The Convoy

Many years after he had left Ards, when the everyday details of the Farm were forgotten, Karl would remember the long, light summer evenings. Even after dank days sodden with rain, in the evenings the wind would drop and the sea would become calm. Above, the heavy clouds would magically drift away, leaving a clear sky glowing with hazy streaks of rosy gold, or scribbled over with the white and grey of a pigeon's wing – a pattern Karl had learned to call mares' tails, or a mackerel sky.

On one of those evenings, on a Saturday not long after the haymaking, Karl found himself alone with Judy outside the Regal Cinema in Donaghadee. A group from the Farm had gone to the pictures, and Karl had come out to the shop to get fish and chips, a favourite treat previously unknown to the refugees. As he turned to go back into the cinema, he bumped into Judy rushing out, and almost dropped the delicious-smelling newspaper-wrapped parcel.

'Not *another* bull after you?' he said.

She laughed. 'It's so hot inside. I was coming out to get ice-cream.'

Something about the luminous evening light and Judy's laughter made Karl say, suddenly carefree, 'Do you want to go back in? It isn't late; maybe we could go for a walk on the beach instead.'

She agreed quickly. 'It wasn't a very good film.'

◆ ❖ ◆

As Karl followed Judy along the narrow grassy path bordering the shore, which led back to Millisle, he noticed that her thick brown hair, instead of being woven into the usual plaits, was caught back loosely with a clip. It made her look older, prettier, especially when she smiled.

He wondered if he would ever be able to tell her about his life. Not about Lisl – that would be too hurtful – but maybe about some of the things that had happened in Vienna, about Uncle Rudi, and poor Goldi, and Tommy and Benji, and his own efforts to help his parents. These were things the refugees spoke of rarely, and only among themselves. How could someone like Judy, with her safe, sheltered life, understand or even be interested in his sorrows and misfortunes?

'By the way,' she was saying, 'did you ever explain to Peewee about synagogues?'

'Well, I tried,' said Karl. 'Tell me, in Dublin, is it important, as it is here, whether you are Protestant or Roman Catholic – or Jewish?'

'Well, my best friend Nora is Catholic.' Judy paused to

consider. 'I suppose it does matter a bit. We all go to our own youth clubs, and Guides and Scouts troops, and church or synagogue. Of course, you can be friends with your neighbours even if they're another religion.' She paused. 'But your parents wouldn't want you to marry out of your faith, though some people do.' She added, 'Isn't it the same in your country?'

How could he begin to explain to her? A bitter note that Judy hadn't heard before crept into Karl's voice. 'Before the Nazis, everyone could be friends–' He stopped. 'But now, everything has changed. To be a Jew, or a Gypsy, is the worst thing. We cannot mix with "Aryans" – people of other religions – or even talk to them.' He paused. 'The Nazis have made us outsiders.' He turned his head away, gazing over the still, silky water that reflected the colours of the sky, scowling to stop the sudden gush of anger that had caught him unawares.

Judy didn't know what to say. The things he was talking about had sometimes been mentioned at home. But in Karl's words, they seemed to take on a new, harsh reality.

Karl tried to collect himself. Drawing a deep breath, he said, 'I'm sorry. We were talking about Ireland. Here in Ards, I think there are hardly any Jews.'

'I suppose that's why people are surprised, like Peewee,' said Judy.

'Yes, but many people here have been very kind to us,' said Karl. 'They do not make a fuss, but they do good things quietly, to help. Still, a few people are – what is the word? – sus–'

'Suspicious?' said Judy.

He nodded. 'Because we speak German and we have different customs. Police in plain clothes have been to look around the Farm.' He gave an ironic smile. 'They think some of us could be spies.'

'You're joking!' said Judy.

Karl shook his head.

'Well,' she went on, 'at least Peewee's family don't think you're a spy, otherwise they wouldn't have asked us to tea next week.'

Karl nodded. It was better to talk to her about the present, about here, he thought, rather than about the past, and there. This was the first time he had talked properly, in English, to a girl who was not a fellow refugee. And, apart from that one moment when he had lost control, it was going quite well.

❖ ❖ ❖

As they strolled along, Judy stole a glance at Karl. When he wasn't smiling there was a sad droop to his mouth. Although she knew he was anxious about his sister, she had also become aware that all the people on the farm – even Gaby, she supposed – had tragic stories. What was Karl's story? And who was the mysterious Lisl? That comment about being an outsider was the only hint he'd ever given her. And then he'd withdrawn behind the barrier that stopped anyone getting too close. Would she ever break through and find out the truth about him?

Meanwhile they talked about the Farm, and the new foal, which everyone had been to the stable to inspect, as it gazed around with huge, wondering eyes, trembling on unsteady legs.

'Will it be all right?' Judy asked Karl. 'It's so tiny and help-less.'

'It is sweet,' he said. 'I must show it to Rosa on her next visit.' He went on, 'But Peewee told me that sometimes, if they're born too early, they cannot suck the mother's milk properly. Mr Teevan told Gaby to feed it with a baby's bottle.'

'*Gaby?*' said Judy, surprised.

'Yes,' said Karl, 'I know it's odd, but he is good with ani-mals.'

Changing the subject, he asked Judy about her life in Dublin, and she started to tell him about her school, and Til-ly's illness, and about how she herself always seemed to be in trouble at home. Karl listened hungrily to her tales of fam-ily life until they reached the beach below Millisle.

Apart from a few families folding up deckchairs and gath-ering buckets and spades, the beach was almost deserted. Karl and Judy walked barefoot, avoiding the rocks, squelch-ing their toes into the spaghetti-like worm casts and the remains of sandcastles, fast disappearing with the incoming tide. Judy squealed as icy wavelets crept over her ankles and then retreated, leaving an expanse of clean wet sand stud-ded with shining stones and shells and draped with slimy strings of browny-green seaweed.

'This is much better than a stuffy cinema,' she said to Karl, breathing in the fresh salt-smell of the sea, as they examined tiny crabs and a dead starfish.

Karl stared out to sea. 'It is so clear! You can see Scotland.'

They gazed at the distant tracing on the horizon. Then

Karl pointed to larger smudges, closer to them, moving. Shading his eyes, he could just make out a series of huge ghostly ships steaming slowly from right to left, parallel with the shore.

'It's a convoy,' he said, 'of warships.'

'How can you see that?' Judy said. 'You must have amazing eyesight.'

'It must be going to the Clyde harbour–'

'Judy, Karl!' someone called. Norman, his trousers rolled up to his knees, his brown jacket over his arm, was walking along the beach with Susi, lecturing her about something.

'What are you doing here?' Judy asked him. Karl could tell she wasn't too pleased to see Norman. And it was unusual to see Susi without the watchful presence of Rina.

Susi showed them a paper bag filled with a variety of shells – white-tipped black mussels, long twin-jointed oyster shells, tiny pink ovals, frilly curved ones with razor edges. 'Norman is helping me collect them. I am making a shell-box for my mother,' she said. 'It is soon her birthday.'

Judy admired the shells, but Karl remained silent. He knew that Susi's mother was in prison, and she was unlikely to see the shell-box for a long time.

'Did you see the convoy?' asked Norman. Fishing a small pair of binoculars out of his bulging pocket, he held them out. 'They're my dad's,' he explained. 'He uses them for the races. You get a great view.'

'Maybe we shouldn't use these,' said Karl uneasily. 'We aren't supposed to do anything which would make people suspicious.'

'Oh, come on, Karl, that's crazy,' said Norman. 'Anyway,

we're from Dublin; no one's going to question us.'

Karl shrugged, still worried; but he didn't want Norman to sneer at him, or Judy to think he was timid.

They each gazed in turn through the binoculars.

'Well, they may be good for the races,' said Judy, 'but all I can see is a winking light.'

'You're looking in the wrong direction,' said Norman. 'That's the Donaghadee lighthouse.' He focused on the ships. 'There's thick smoke coming from two of them,' he said. 'And one is a long way behind.'

'They must have been damaged,' said Karl, 'perhaps by U-boats, or bombers.'

Susi shivered. 'Soldiers or sailors might have been hurt, or killed, on those ships.'

The dark shadow of the war, never far away for the refugees, drew closer.

◆ ❖ ◆

That night, Karl was woken by voices and footsteps in the farmyard. Everyone else in the dormitory was asleep. Outside, a pinpoint of light moved as someone held a torch.

He wondered if it had anything to do with the foal, which he knew had grown weaker. Pulling on his clothes, he slipped out into the darkness and crept round the back of the wooden buildings to the office window, where a chink of light showed through a gap in the blackout curtains.

Inside he could see Mr Senesh, a coat over his pyjamas, and two other men. One was in police uniform, but it wasn't their local Sergeant O'Connor, the ruddy-faced man who issued the travel permits; this man was a stranger.

Mrs Franck, in a blue dressing-gown, her hair down, hurried past without seeing Karl, and went inside.

'What's going on?' Danny was crouching beside him.

Karl shrugged. Through the thin wooden wall they could hear Mr Senesh saying, 'There must be a mistake. All the older boys here have appeared before the board in Newtownards and have permits to be in a coastal area–'

'That may be,' said the officer heavily. 'But we've had reports that someone may have been signalling to enemy ships or U-boats from the beach.' He paused. 'It seems they had binoculars.'

Karl froze.

'That's not possible, officer,' came Mrs Franck's low voice. 'We refugees have only a few clothes and possessions. No one has binoculars.'

'Did you hear?' Karl whispered to Danny. 'It's about us. I was on the beach watching the convoy with Norman. He had binoculars. We all used them.'

'Fool!' hissed Danny. 'You know we're not even supposed to sit on the sea wall–'

'Should I tell them?'

Inside, Mrs Franck was saying, 'Could we call Sergeant O'Connor? He'll confirm that we have always been very careful to cooperate with the authorities.'

'He is off duty. You'll have to deal with me.'

Danny gave Karl a nudge. 'It sounds serious. You'd better go in and explain, or we'll all be carted off to prison for spying.'

Karl hoped he was joking. Bracing himself, he knocked on the office door.

26

Spies!

When Judy came in to breakfast the next morning, wild rumours about the previous night's events were buzzing around. Neither Karl nor Norman was there; nor were any of the adults.

Eva looked agitated. 'Have you heard?' she said. 'Norman and Karl have been arrested for spying.'

'Spying?' said Judy. 'That's ridiculous.' But she was perturbed to see Susi in floods of tears, and the older ones with worried expressions.

'It is serious,' said Gaby grimly. 'They haven't actually been arrested, but they are being questioned in the police station.' He glared at Judy. 'Karl – and the rest of us – could end up in an internment camp.'

'What were you all doing on the beach, anyway?' said Rina angrily. 'Susi should not have gone with Norman. He thinks he knows so much, but he does not understand things here. To the police, we are enemy aliens. And now we are all in trouble.'

Unusually, Judy did not snap back at her. Rina had a point. Judy recalled Karl's concern about the binoculars, and how she had ignored him and Norman had sneered.

Supposing Karl was interned, like so many other refugees? What would happen to Rosa? And Norman, and she herself, might be sent back to Dublin. Once she would have jumped at the chance. But, she realised, not any more.

◆ ❖ ◆

At lunch, Karl and Norman finally appeared. They were greeted with relief, and a few ironic cheers.

Karl, Judy thought, appeared pale and subdued, dark rings under his eyes, his smile missing. He said little, and Norman, full of self-importance, did most of the talking.

'The RUC officer asked to see my binoculars,' he told them, 'and they wanted to know where I got them, and what we were looking at. Of course,' he added, 'once I explained, and showed my passport and they saw I was only visiting the Farm from Dublin, it was fine. They were more interested in Karl.' He sounded slightly aggrieved. 'They spent ages examining his papers and his registration book, and asking where he was from, and how he got to Millisle, and what he did on the Farm.'

'How did they treat you?' Danny asked Karl quietly.

'They were polite,' said Karl. 'It was not like–' He stopped. 'Mr Senesh explained most things to them. But all the questions made me nervous, and I kept forgetting my English ...' His voice died away.

Norman went on to explain that, on the insistence of Mr

Senesh, Sergeant O'Connor had been called from home. With his arrival, the matter had rapidly been sorted out. Karl, Norman and Mr Senesh had been allowed to leave, with handshakes all round.

As Norman held forth, Judy looked at Karl's drawn face, and her heart clenched with sympathy for him. For the first time she glimpsed what it meant to be – as Karl had once described – an outsider, alone, not to be a citizen of any country, not to have your parents to turn to. Judy knew that if she or Norman or Pearl were ever in serious trouble, their families would be there. For the refugees, if they were lucky, there might be committees, and perhaps people like Mr Senesh and Yakobi. But they had no one, and no place, of their own.

◆ ❖ ◆

That evening, Mr Senesh made a short speech warning everyone not to sit on the sea wall, or go to the beach in the evenings, or even stare out to sea. 'These rules are for everybody, for those from Dublin also,' he said. 'Although what happened was an unfortunate misunderstanding, it is still important we do not upset the people here, who have welcomed us and helped us.'

As they left the dining hall, Norman muttered to Judy, 'Those rules are pretty stupid.'

Yakobi overheard. He said sharply, without his usual smile, 'When people are fighting a desperate war, they can get very jumpy.' He continued, with emphasis, 'It is quiet here now, but one day the war will come, even to beautiful

Ards. So we must be always careful. You understand?'

They nodded silently, and he walked away.

They exchanged uncomfortable glances. Even Norman looked sheepish.

After a moment, Pearl said fearfully, 'Do you think he means we'll be invaded, or bombed?'

'My uncle in Belfast says no one expects the North to be bombed,' said Norman. But he sounded less confident than usual.

'In the letter I just got from home,' said Judy, 'my brother says there couldn't be air raids here. It's too far for the German bombers, and anyway, all their sights are set on England.'

'But if the Nazis *did* come here–' Pearl stopped. 'D'you know, in the dairy one day, Rina told me this awful story about Nazi officers calling to their home in Berlin and ransacking the apartment. Rina came home from school to find Susi hysterical, and their parents gone. They'd been taken to prison.'

They were all silent. Judy asked, 'What happened then?'

'They haven't seen their parents since that day, not even to say goodbye when they left on the Kindertransport.'

Judy shivered. Was this the kind of thing that had happened to Karl and the others? Could it happen one day to Pearl, to Norman – to her?

27

The Ulster Tea

The police questioning, civil though it was, had dredged up buried fears from Karl's Vienna days. For some time afterwards, he woke early in the mornings, unsettled by half-remembered dreams of hostile SS guards and rampaging Hitler Youth.

He tried to push away the dark memories, as he and Judy waited for Peewee outside Borza's Ice-Cream Parlour in Millisle village. The Farm children often went there to buy wafers and cones, which they had learned to call 'sliders' and 'pokes'. With the last of her wages, Judy bought them each a penny poke.

It was a warm, cloudless day. They stood in the shade of the shop's striped awning, savouring the rich sweetness of the yellowy home-made ice-cream. Karl pointed across at the village school. 'That's where I went for my first few months here, till I turned fourteen. The teacher sat each of us with a local child to help us learn English.'

'Who were you with?'

'Bobby Hackett,' said Karl. 'He was friendly to me. On the first day he showed me that he has six fingers on each hand. I never forgot this!' He grinned. 'And he's a good footballer. He'll be playing against us in the match.'

'What school do you go to now?' asked Judy.

'Yakobi asked at the schools in Newtownards and Bangor, whether they would take us older ones. So, thanks to him, I go to Bangor High. My teacher, Mr Armstrong, helped me. Sometime I'll show you the Irish poem he wrote in my autograph book.'

They heard a piping whistle, like a blackbird's. Judy shaded her eyes to peer down the village street, chequered with wedges of vivid sunlight, and deep shadow under the awnings.

Peewee, perched on a heavy old delivery bike, was wobbling towards them. 'I hope you're good and hungry,' he said, when he reached them. 'My ma has a feast ready – potato cakes and all. But,' he added, his blue eyes dancing, 'no hang sandwiches.'

He turned to Judy. 'And don't mind Granny. She's a bit sharp, like, specially if you're from the South. It's just her way.'

Judy threw Karl a nervous glance as they followed Peewee down the laneway and into the cobbled yard of Crawford's pub.

◆ ❖ ◆

In the airy, stone-floored kitchen, Peewee's mother, a cheerful, rosy-cheeked woman in a floral apron, stood at the range, which threw out a great heat despite the warmth of the day.

'Pleased to meet you,' she said. Karl held out his hand, and she shook it, surprised. 'Such nice manners!'

As they sat around the scrubbed deal table, she went on, 'Peewee tells me ye've had a hard time.'

'Not me,' said Judy quickly. 'I'm not a refugee. I'm from Dublin.'

From the fireplace, a cracked voice said, 'Which is the wean from Dublin?'

They turned to see a figure so small and withered that she was lost in the cushioned armchair, like a tiny baby in a big cradle. They could see beady eyes in a wrinkled face, framed by a few strands of thin silvery hair, through which pink scalp peeped.

Peewee said in resigned tones, 'This is my granny.'

Peewee's granny regarded Judy suspiciously. 'From Dublin, are you?' she muttered. 'So what brings you up here?'

Judy summoned up her courage. 'I've come to help the refugees on Millisle Farm.'

'That foreign crowd? And where are they from, when they're at home?' the old lady retorted.

Karl said politely, 'I am from Vienna, and some are from Germany, and from Prague.'

Granny regarded them piercingly, then said unexpectedly, 'Sure, of course ye're welcome here, young weans away from their home. But I've not seen any of ye in the church of a Sunday–' She was overcome by a fit of coughing.

Mrs Crawford quickly put in, 'Granny, d'you mind how Granda used to say a person's religion was their private business?'

Granny subsided, darting a sharp glance at Judy.

In a whisper, Mrs Crawford confided to them, 'Granny's bark's worse than her bite.' While Karl tried to puzzle out what that could mean, she went on, 'I think we'll have tea. Wee Billy has a few hours' leave, but he may be late. And my husband is busy in the bar.'

Pouring the tea, Mrs Crawford chatted on about rationing, the shortages of white flour and tinned fruit, the nuisance of the blackout. 'We're all knitting comforts for the troops – socks and mufflers and suchlike,' she told them.

'I mind the socks we knitted for the last war, the Great War,' Granny put in. 'Didn't do them much good in the trenches or at the Somme, poor wee craturs.'

'That was a terrible war,' said Mrs Crawford.

'All the wars are terrible,' grunted Granny.

Mrs Crawford sighed. 'Aye, so they are. You'd wish we didn't–' She stopped.

'Mammy, we have to fight Hitler,' put in Peewee. 'That's what Wee Billy says.' At the mention of her soldier son, his mother lit up with pride, and Granny's face softened.

◆ ❖ ◆

What a tea, thought Karl, savouring the delicious floury soda farls, the warm potato-cakes soaked in melting butter, the tomato sandwiches, the nutty brown scones with home-made jam.

Despite her rheumy cough, Granny ate with relish. 'Only time you get a decent tea's when there's visitors,' she mumbled. She appeared to have trouble with her false teeth, and at one point she took them out and placed them on her plate. 'Useless!' she grunted.

'Now, Gran,' said Mrs Crawford, smiling apologetically at Judy and Karl.

'My granny in Dublin has trouble with her teeth as well,' said Judy consolingly.

Mrs Crawford poured more tea. 'I'm glad Peewee's found friends,' she said to Judy and Karl. 'And he's that excited about the match! It hasn't been easy for him here. Country folk can be suspicious of strangers. And we're still only finding our way.'

'When we first came here to the pub, we kept getting lost,' grinned Peewee.

'Where we lived before,' said his mother, 'we had just two wee rooms up and two down, and an outside privy.'

'Do you like it better here?' asked Judy.

'Aye, I do,' said Peewee, 'but sometimes I miss my pals.'

'In Belfast, I did a bit of nursing, and my husband was unemployed,' said Mrs Crawford, 'so this pub's something new for all of us.'

Granny finished her potato cake, put her teeth back in and began to tell them about her days in the York Street Mill.

'The young weans today'll never understand,' she said. 'We worked in the mill from the age of ten, starting at dawn when the first tram left. When you got to the mill on the frosty dark mornings, it was all lit up, but it was fierce cold inside – you could see your breath. And all the girls would come hurrying in, pulling their shawls round them, their clogs clacking on the stone floor ...' She paused, remembering. 'Then the machines would start humming, and we'd set to work. Us weans would run to help the spinners–' Her frail body shook with a violent series of coughs.

'It's the powse makes her cough,' said Mrs Crawford. 'The white dust off the linen cloth. It gets into everyone's lungs, especially in the winter when you can't open the windows in the mill. That stuff harms you forever.'

'I hope you've left a wee bit of food for a starving soldier,' said a voice. An immensely tall young man in uniform had appeared in the doorway. He had the same sandy hair and colouring as Peewee, but a more serious expression.

Mrs Crawford had to stand on tiptoe to hug him. As the soldier bent to kiss his granny, Karl said to Peewee incredulously, 'Is *that* Wee Billy?'

Peewee grinned broadly. 'That's Wee Billy.'

◆ ❖ ◆

After Wee Billy's arrival, they all lingered around the table. Eating steadily, Billy answered Karl's eager questions about his training with the Inniskilling Fusiliers, and told them about his ambition to fight in the front line. At these words, Mrs Crawford closed her eyes for a second, though she said nothing.

Wee Billy turned to Karl and Judy. 'Peewee tells me you've a tricky football match coming up,' he said. 'D'you need a hand?'

'Billy's a champion player,' Peewee put in proudly.

'Our team badly needs help,' said Karl.

Billy nodded amiably. 'I'll do what I can.'

In the flurry of their departure, a memory kept slithering

into Karl's mind – the dining-table at home, and everyone sitting around it – a family gathering, like this one, but a world away. He gave himself a tiny shake, and Wee Billy, noticing, asked kindly, 'Were you dreaming, young fella?'

'Poor wee lad, away from his family,' said Mrs Crawford. 'He has a lot to worry about, so he has.'

Before they left, they went into the bar to see Peewee's father, a thin, solemn-faced man in a dark suit, busy at the polished mahogany counter. Behind him the mirrored shelves reflected countless glasses and bottles and advertisements for Comber Distilleries and Jameson's Whiskey, and one that said, 'Guinness is Good for You'.

Mr Crawford nodded to them politely enough, but something in his manner made Karl wonder if perhaps he was not entirely happy about Peewee's new friends.

28

Air-Raid Warning

A few mornings after tea at the Crawfords', the Postilion handed Karl not one letter, but two, saying, 'Good news, I think.' Karl felt a rare flash of hope as he opened the thin air-mail envelope, with its unfamiliar foreign stamp, and turned over the single sheet inside. The signature jumped out at him: Tommy.

Tommy's letter explained that he had been smuggled out of Vienna a few months previously, with a group of other young refugees. After a dangerous journey, he had eventually made it to Palestine, where he was living in a youth village.

The family were all right when I left Vienna, Tommy wrote, *but things are bad there, and everyone's sad about Uncle Rudi. It was hard to leave Benji behind, but they said he was too young for the journey.*

Because of all the censorship, it's almost impossible to get anything out of Austria. It was too dangerous for me even to carry a letter from your mother, in case I was searched. I've memorised the address of her cousin in America for you, even though she said they haven't been able to get in touch with her.

A lot of Jews are being forced to travel east (that ominous phrase again, thought Karl), *and I was lucky to escape. It's good here, but I'm lonely sometimes. Write and tell me what it's like in Millisle. How's Rosa? It will be great when we can see each other and our families again, when the war is over.*

For a moment, Karl felt cheered. Although Tommy was so far away, at least he was safe. But Benji and the others were not. Karl sighed and turned to the other letter. It was from one of the refugee aid organisations he had written to. To his delight, this one – unlike the others – said that a few visas for Australia or Hong Kong might be available, but that a lot of money would be needed to bribe Nazi officials. Although these things were very difficult, if Karl had any relations who could help, the organisation would try to get the money to his family in Vienna, and help make arrangements.

Karl decided he would write to this unknown American cousin at once, asking for help for his parents. Any destination would do, as long as they got out of Nazi hands. And he would write back to Tommy, too, right away.

Half an hour later, his letters written and his heart lighter, he went to help Danny paint the wings of the model Spitfire, and to discuss their team's prospects now that a champion footballer might be coming to their aid.

◆ ❖ ◆

That night, Judy was woken by an eerie sound, a persistent mechanical wail that rose and fell. She had been in a deep sleep, having stayed up late telling Pearl and Eva about the Crawfords and Wee Billy.

As Judy struggled awake, Rina, in a threadbare dressing-gown, hurried over to the window. Twitching apart the heavy blackout curtains, she peered through the tiny gap.

'What's that awful noise?' asked Judy, yawning.

'I think it's a siren,' said Rina slowly. 'It must be an air-raid warning.'

They stared at each other. Pearl, pale as a ghost, leaped out of bed. Judy felt a prickle of fear. Surely they weren't going to be bombed after all?

By now, everyone in the dormitory was up, some of the younger ones whimpering

'What shall we do?' gasped Pearl.

'Quick,' said Eva, 'get their coats and gas masks. We must shelter in the big barn.' They rushed around, too busy to panic, Pearl murmuring a prayer under her breath.

Outside there was pandemonium. Everyone poured out of the dormitories in nightclothes, clutching coats and gas masks. People were milling around and children were crying. 'Put out those lights!' someone roared. 'Remember the black-out.' Above, searchlights criss-crossed the inky sky, but all was quiet.

Mr Senesh and Yakobi, carrying dimmed torches, were directing everyone to the barn. Stumbling in her slippers on the slippery cobbles, Judy felt a squelch as she trod in a cow-clap. Then someone called her name. It was Karl, with Danny and Norman. In shrunken pyjamas and an old, darned jersey, with his hair ruffled from sleep, he looked somehow younger and a bit pathetic.

They crammed into the barn, which smelled of oily machinery and dried hay. Judy spotted Yakobi shepherding two small boys – the one who cried a lot, and the mischievous one, who, Judy recalled, had been playing monopoly that first night. He grinned, as though he was enjoying the fun.

For the first hour, the adults and older refugees were kept busy trying to distract the younger ones. Judy found herself, shivering with nerves, playing an interminable game of 'I-spy' with the little girls from her dormitory. Nearby, a boy was hugging the Farm dog, who usually slept on his bed; Gaby, tousled and handsome, sat with his arm around one of the older girls.

Prayers were recited, and a psalm that Judy recognised, 'The Lord is my shepherd.' After a while people started singing, Mr Senesh's booming voice roaring out the chorus of an Austrian mountain song, 'Valdari, valdara ...' Encouraged by Yakobi, Norman led the Dublin crowd in a faltering version of 'Molly Malone', which the refugees listened to politely and uncomprehendingly.

And all the time they listened nervously, with half an ear, for the sound of plane-engines or explosions.

The time dragged by. Some of the younger children fell asleep on the rough wooden benches. A few boys, including Karl and Danny, played card games. One or two couples among the older refugees sat close to each other, whispering and holding hands.

Judy and the other girls conversed quietly. Rina, Judy noticed, seemed softer and friendlier, less prickly, with this sharing of common danger.

In a quiet corner of the barn, Yakobi had soothed the little crying boy to an occasional whimper.

'Poor little thing,' said Eva. 'I believe he has had a bad time.'

'He was beaten by Hitler Youth thugs, and forced to paint "Jude" – that is "Jew" – on a shop window,' said Rina, in a low voice. 'He cries all the time for home.'

Recalling with embarrassment her own tactless comment about the weeping child, Judy said nothing.

Pearl said, 'Yakobi is very kind, isn't he?'

The others nodded. 'Mr Senesh is more strict, but strong, like a rock,' said Rina. 'We can depend on him, and on the Francks.'

'And Mr Freeman and the other Belfast people do much for us,' said Eva. 'But mostly, with our own troubles, we go to Yakobi. He always listens.'

'But he can get angry,' said Rina, 'when people are ignorant about the war–'

As she spoke, the single high note of a siren sounded in the distance. A buzz of relieved chatter burst out.

'The all-clear,' shouted Norman. 'Must've been a false alarm.'

◆ ❖ ◆

Before they left the barn, Mr Senesh announced that in future there would be regular air-raid practices on the Farm. He went on, 'I hope to see *all* of you in the synagogue next Sabbath, to give thanks for our safety.'

Back in bed, Judy thought that, although there had been

no raid, the war had suddenly lurched closer to them. Her mouth was still dry with fear, which she realised must be a familiar feeling to the refugees. Could there ever be a real air raid at the Farm – an air raid like the ones they had seen on the cinema newsreels, with death and destruction raining from the sky? Surely everyone who insisted that Ireland was safe couldn't be wrong?

But as she drifted off to sleep, Yakobi's words echoed in her mind: 'The war will come here one day, even to beautiful Ards.'

29

Football Practice

Two days later, Judy and Pearl were watching the football practice. Even Judy, who was no expert, could see it wasn't going well. Gaby, the eldest in the team, had insisted on being on the wing. He hogged the ball while the other players ran aimlessly up and down the field, waiting hopefully for a bit of action, which never came. Then one of the older refugees, who had half-heartedly acted as coach, left, saying he had to fix a broken washing machine. The game wavered to a halt.

'They're not much of a team,' Judy said to Pearl.

Pearl wasn't listening. She was gazing at Danny with a moony look – rather like one of the cows, Judy thought nastily. Everyone knew Pearl admired Danny, and blushed whenever he talked to her; but it was a bit late for her to get really interested in him now, when it was nearly time for them to go back to Dublin.

The days on the farm, which at first had seemed to stretch ahead endlessly, were slipping by faster and faster, like a speeded-up film. Judy could not imagine going back to her old, boring life. Even seeing Nora again was no compensation for leaving the Farm, the refugees – and Karl. Once they left Millisle, would she ever see him again?

And then, just as the football practice was breaking up and the downhearted players and spectators were about to walk off, a voice shouted, 'Where's this famous team, then?'

They all looked up as Wee Billy came striding across the field, looking eager, and somehow younger and more approachable out of uniform. Peewee raced over to him. 'It's not going great,' he told Billy. 'We've no coach.'

Instantly assessing the situation, Billy peeled off his jacket and ran onto the roughly marked pitch. Within minutes he had reassembled all the players and got the game going. Then, after a short conference on the pitch, he re-arranged the team, placing Peewee on the wing, Karl as centre-half, Norman inside, and Gaby – who was plainly annoyed by the new arrival – in goal. The practice resumed, with Billy himself in the middle of things, maintaining the pace and keeping an eye on the ball.

The spectators along the pitch perked up. 'Well,' said Pearl, taking her eyes off Danny with an effort, 'looks like they've got a new coach.'

On the pitch Wee Billy shouted, 'C'mon, now, all of ye. Eyes on the ball!'

Walking back after the practice behind Wee Billy, who was deep in conversation with Yakobi, there was a newly confident air among players and spectators.

'Best practice we've had,' said Danny cheerily. 'That Billy's some coach, to do anything with this lot.'

'He is that,' agreed Peewee. 'Hey, did you hear the air-raid warning?'

'We all sheltered in the hay-barn,' Pearl told him.

'We went down to the cellar,' said Peewee. 'But Granny stayed put. She said it would take more than rotten old Hitler to move her out of her warm bed.'

Judy grinned. 'I'll bet she did.'

'D'you think our team will do all right?' Pearl, blushing, asked Danny as he walked beside her.

He pushed back his fair hair, smiling. 'With luck.'

'And with a good centre forward,' added Karl. 'If we could find one.'

As they passed the clucking cacophony of the hen-house, Grace Doherty waved to them. 'Hello, there. When are you coming back to help with the hens, Judy?'

Although Judy had been allocated a variety of jobs during her time on the Farm, she had never forgotten that first woeful day in the hen-house. 'Um, I'm not sure,' she said. 'Mr Senesh said I should try milking before I go back.'

'Pity,' said Grace, with an ironic grin. 'I'm sure I could have made a good hen-woman out of you – eventually.' She turned to Karl. 'By the way, I hear you need someone for the team.'

He nodded. 'We have now a great new coach, but we're still short of players.'

'Well, maybe this is out of line, but I'm a player myself. I've five older brothers who play. I'd help out if you're stuck.'

There was an astonished silence. Finally Peewee ventured, 'I never heard of ladies playing football.'

Grace laughed her rich laugh. 'A lady? Sure, I'm only eighteen. When's the match?'

'That's a problem,' said Karl. 'We cannot play on Saturdays, our Sabbath. Peewee and Billy cannot play on Sundays. And we must have it soon, before the Dublin people go back.' He paused. 'But thank you for offering to play. I will speak to Wee Billy.'

30

War News

At supper, everyone wanted to talk to Wee Billy, who along with Peewee had been invited to stay for the meal. Even Gaby had a few polite words with Billy about the game, before going off to check on the sick foal. Watching him hurry away, Judy reflected that though Gaby had so many girl-friends, he seemed to care more for animals than people.

In the rec, Eva and Rina put on swing records, and Yakobi played a game of billiards with Wee Billy.

'It is good of you to help our team,' Yakobi told him, across the billiard table.

Lining up his shot, Wee Billy grinned. 'They sure need help.' He added quickly, 'But they'll be a fine team.'

At nine o'clock, the radio news came on. Nazi U-boats were torpedoing ships in the English Channel, and there had been heavy air raids on the south of England.

'It is not so far from us,' said Rina with a shiver, as they clustered around the war map. Recalling her story, Judy regarded her, for the first time, with sympathy.

'How long do you think the war will last?' Danny asked Wee Billy. The word had flashed round that Billy, as well as being their new football coach, was also a soldier.

'They say it'll be a long, hard struggle,' said Billy.

'Will you be fighting in Europe when your training is finished?' Rina asked him, in a rare tone of respect.

'Our ma doesn't want Billy to be in the front line,' Peewee blurted out. 'She says she knows it's hard for the refugees, but she wishes we could just stay out of the war.'

Billy threw him a look. For a brief moment, no one spoke.

Then Yakobi said, 'War brings always sorrow and destruction. And for a mother, especially, it is terrible.' He glanced down at the sad little boy sitting silently beside him, and they could feel the force behind his words. 'We all want peace. But for us refugees, there is no choice about this war.'

Karl, changing the gramophone needle, looked up. 'It is not just the refugees' war. It's everyone's war, even here in Ireland,' he murmured. 'A war for ...'

Judy saw that, in his agitation, his English had failed him. A remembered phrase flashed into her mind, and she put in quickly, 'A war for decency, my da says.' Karl glanced at her gratefully.

'Most of us here will fight as soon as we can,' put in Danny, unusually serious. 'I also want to be in the front line.'

Yakobi said gently to Peewee. 'I would like to explain to your mother, that if an evil leader like Hitler conquers the whole of Europe, and he and his fellow Nazis enslave and destroy–'

'And drive people from their homes, just because of their race or religion–' said Danny.

'And torture and murder innocent people–' put in Rina, her voice trembling.

'Then decent people cannot stand by and hope they will just go away,' continued Yakobi. 'If a bully will not listen to reason, there comes a time when you have to stand up to him.'

Wee Billy looked round the room at the children, most of them torn from their families and uprooted from their homes. He put his hand on Peewee's shoulder. 'I understand how my ma feels,' he said quietly, 'And everyone else's mother, and Eileen–'

'Of course,' said Yakobi. 'But we must remember,' he went on with rare firmness, 'that this evil hatred and prejudice can happen anywhere, not just in Nazi Germany or Austria. And wherever it does, it must be stopped.'

Billy nodded agreement. 'Sometimes,' he said, 'sometimes, you have to fight.'

The door of the rec flew open, and a small boy burst in. 'Mr Senesh wants Karl Muller,' he said importantly. 'There is a telephone call.'

A phone call at Millisle was a rarity. Karl jumped to his feet, his heart racing. Could it be good news? No, it was more likely to be bad ...

He ran to the office, knocked hastily, and entered.

Mr Senesh was at his desk. 'Karl,' he said, 'Mr Gould phoned. It is your sister Rosa. I'm afraid she has had an accident.'

31

The Accident

Fifty pairs of eyes stared as Karl, accompanied by Yakobi, tip-toed into the gloomy women's ward of Newtownards Hospital. Flushed with anxiety and embarrassment, he scanned the long rows of iron beds.

He finally spotted Rosa – a small, vulnerable figure, one leg in heavy white plaster, her face tearstained, her ringlets tangled and dull.

Mrs Gould was sitting on a chair by the bed. At the sight of Karl, she stood up. 'Rosa, dear, your brother has come to see you. Now you'll feel better.'

Karl, hugging his sister to him, felt her body trembling with suppressed sobs.

Yakobi turned to Mrs Gould. 'What happened?'

'Poor darling,' said Mrs Gould, dabbing at her eyes with a lace handkerchief. 'For a special treat, we took her skating, and she fell.' She made a face at them and mouthed 'broken ankle'.

'Poor Rosa,' said Karl softly. 'Is it very sore?'

She nodded, tears trickling down her cheeks.

'She's not speaking much.' Mrs Gould turned to the child. 'But guess what I've got for our little Rosa.' Reaching into a bag, she produced two bars of KitKat, rarely seen since the war began. 'This is a whole month's ration!'

Rosa stared at the chocolate without a word.

'And see what else I've brought!' Mrs Gould fished in the bag and triumphantly held out the new doll, which she and her husband had given Rosa in the Belfast hostel.

Rosa slowly reached out for it. Then her face contorted, and with a violent movement she hurled it to the floor. The smiling china face smashed to pieces.

There was a sudden hush in the ward. All eyes turned towards them. A nurse hurried over.

'Rosa!' cried Mrs Gould. 'How could you? Your lovely doll ...'

'I don't want *that* doll!' Rosa shouted. 'I want my real doll, Mitzi, from home. And I want my Mama.' And she burst into noisy sobs, burying her face in Karl's jersey, just as Mr Gould appeared with a bunch of flowers.

◆ ❖ ◆

Later, back in the farm cart beside Yakobi, Karl gazed at the bulky, reassuring hindquarters of Jean, the workhorse, trotting back to Millisle. Battling with his pity and concern for Rosa, he felt a dull anger at this new problem facing him.

'It's not fair,' he told Yakobi, lapsing into German. 'I love Rosa dearly. But I have to be a father and a mother to her. And what with everything else, and trying to help my parents ... it's just too much.'

'You're right. It's not fair.' Yakobi held the horse's reins loosely. 'It's the war that forces you to take on such heavy responsibilities when you're so young.' Seeing Karl's clenched fists, he went on, 'You can be angry, Karl. You mustn't try to keep everything inside you.' He paused. 'I'm often angry myself, about everything that's happened to us. When I feel like that, I play my saxophone.'

'Does it help?' asked Karl.

Yakobi shrugged. 'The sax was the only thing I was able to bring with me from home,' he said. 'But I play less and less. It was part of my other life, the life that's gone. Now we have to think about the future, not the past.'

Around them in the violet dusk, trees and bushes stood out like black cut-outs. Karl's mind was still on Rosa. 'As soon as she can walk, I must get her to the Farm,' he told Yakobi fiercely, 'even if the Goulds don't agree. I know they're doing their best, but they're just smothering her with kindness and toys, and she's not happy.'

After a moment, Yakobi said, 'I believe for many years the Goulds wished for a child of their own. That may be why they try too hard and are too protective.' The cart rattled into the yard of the Farm. He went on, 'It's sad – I think they mean well.'

'Maybe,' said Karl, too angry and upset to feel pity for the Goulds. 'But I have to put Rosa first.'

As they climbed down from the cart, Yakobi said quietly, 'I can see that Rosa should be here with you. We'll talk to Anton Senesh.' He patted Karl's rigid shoulder. Then he unhitched Jean and led her into the stable.

In the darkness of the farmyard, a sliver of light showed for an instant as the door of the rec opened and shut. A figure emerged, barely visible in the gloom. Somehow Karl knew straightaway that it was Judy.

She took a few steps towards him. 'Karl? I was just off to bed. How's Rosa?'

Karl fought to keep his voice normal. 'She has a broken ankle.'

'Oh, that's awful,' said Judy.

'She will be all right, but she is not herself.' He brushed a hand across his eyes. Telling her the details, he felt comforted, just by her staying close to him and listening. Then he said, 'I suppose the others have gone?'

'Yes,' said Judy. 'They were really sorry about Rosa. Peewee wanted to wait for you, but they had to get home before the blackout.'

She paused, wondering whether to tell him more bad news. But he would have to hear. 'The foal ...' she began.

'It died?'

She nodded.

'Poor foal,' Karl said. 'Poor Molly, to lose her baby.' He sighed. 'Poor all of us.'

Judy cast around in her mind for something to cheer him. 'Karl, remember the day we were waiting for Peewee? You were going to show me something in your autograph book –'

He brightened. 'I'll get it.'

Returning with the book and a torch a few minutes later, Karl said, 'Let's go to the hatchery. I got the key from Mr Senesh's office.'

The small lean-to shed where baby chicks were hatched

was the only place on the farm that was both warm and private, at least in the evening. Although no one was supposed to go there without permission, it was a popular place for courting couples.

Judy and Karl sat close together on the rough floor, and Karl leafed through the worn leather book. Most of the signatures and verses were in German and meant nothing to Judy.

'When I first went to Bangor High, my teacher, Mr Armstrong, tried to explain to me a little of the history here,' said Karl. 'And he helped me with my English.'

He paused, searching. 'Here's the poem.' He handed the book to Judy. 'Would you like to read it?'

'I – um, yes, of course. Not that I'm much good at poetry.' She began, "Come away, O human child! To the waters and the wild ..." She hesitated.

' "... For the world's more full of weeping,"' Karl continued, ' "–than you can understand."' He went on, 'My teacher told me it was written by an Irish poet, Yeats. And yet it's about us.'

'Us?'

'Us refugees,' he said. 'I often wonder how that poet could understand so well.'

'It's so sad ...' Judy had never considered that a poem could have this sort of personal meaning. 'My autograph book is full of stupid things,' she said, 'like "Roses are red, violets are blue–"' She stopped.

'Yes?'

'"Sugar is sweet, and – so are you,"' she finished, embarrassed. Maybe he thought she was flirting with him. She went on quickly, 'Who gave you your autograph book?'

For a long moment Karl didn't reply. Then he said quietly, 'My uncle Rudi gave it to me, when we left Vienna.'

'Is he still there, with your parents?'

'He is dead,' said Karl flatly. Judy flinched.

Then she told herself that here, at last, was a chance for her to hear his story. Should she probe further? Suddenly she was almost desperate to hear it from him. Maybe he'll tell me about Lisl, she thought. Then I'll really know him.

'Karl,' she said quietly, 'what happened to your uncle Rudi?'

32

The Match

As Judy tramped across the field to the pitch, her mind was crackling with thoughts. The day before, Karl had visited Rosa again, and had found her still very tearful. But, thrilled and relieved, he had told Judy that – after some persuasion from Yakobi and Mr Senesh – the Goulds had reluctantly agreed that a spell at the Farm with Karl might speed Rosa's recovery.

Judy was glad for him, of course. And she had been pleased when, the other evening, in the warmth and quiet of the hatchery, he had told her a little about his experiences in Vienna, about Rudi, and about the miraculous letter from Tommy. She had listened, shocked by the horrors she was hearing; it had been hard to know what to say.

But had Karl's confidences brought them closer, as she had hoped? He hadn't mentioned Lisl. And when Judy had casually asked about her, Karl's face had closed like a trap, all warmth and emotion suddenly hidden. Maybe Karl still cared for Lisl, whoever she was, and just thought of Judy as a casual friend. She wanted to mean more to him than that – to be important to him, as he had become to her.

Beside her, Pearl said sympathetically, 'You're so quiet, Judy. Are you worried about the match? Poor Danny looks worried too.'

With an impatient shrug, Judy bit back a sarcastic reply and turned her attention to the pitch.

◆ ❖ ◆

Nearly everyone at Millisle had knocked off work early. As soon as Wee Billy arrived with Peewee, he got a few players on to the pitch for a last-minute practice. Then the opposing team appeared, led by Karl's old school friend Bobby Hackett.

By the time the game began, in a cold wind, the field was lined with a diverse group of spectators – the Farm children and adults; the older refugees who weren't in the team; the local Farm workers; a few people from the village, and a nearby farmer who was acting as referee.

Both teams had on a variety of scruffy clothes, and most wore their everyday boots. There was a stir when Grace Doherty appeared – at the last minute Wee Billy had agreed to include her, despite his doubts about women playing football. She marched onto the field with the same no-nonsense expression she wore when working with the hens; she was jauntily togged out in a proper striped football shirt and shorts, her abundant coppery hair escaping from its clasp in little tendrils.

'The shirt must be her brother's,' said Judy. 'She really looks the part.'

A few minutes after the match began, Judy heard the sound of a car. She turned to see a strange procession crossing the field. Mrs Crawford and Mr Teevan were supporting Granny, who was wearing a black shawl and an ancient hat with a clump of mouldering feathers. Mrs Crawford threw Judy a smile. Judy could hear Granny quavering, 'There's nothing like getting away out o' the house. And I'm not missing cheering on Peewee and Wee Billy, cough or no cough.'

Out on the pitch, Billy was in the centre of the action, directing play, calling, bellowing and encouraging. But despite his efforts, the ball shot like a bullet past a furious Gaby, giving the village team its first goal. There was a ragged cheer from the sidelines.

Play moved up and down the pitch. Then Peewee, on the wing, headed the ball to Norman, who was playing inside. To everyone's surprise, Norman kicked the ball in a soaring arc towards the goal. But the cheers of the Farm supporters quickly died away as Bobby Hackett, the village team's energetic goalie, easily stopped the ball.

Granny, undaunted, could be heard shouting, 'G'wan, Peewee, you're doing great!' Billy and Peewee heard the familiar croak, and both grinned as they spotted Granny, waving wildly.

When Judy glanced back at the goal, the ball seemed to have appeared from nowhere. Gaby flung himself at it, but it whizzed past him into the net, giving the village team a second goal. There was another cheer, mixed with a groan of disappointment.

Then it was half-time.

'Isn't it a shame?' said Pearl. 'I thought Gaby was supposed to be such a good player.'

'Well, he thinks he is,' said Judy. She looked over at the Crawfords. 'Back in a moment,' she murmured to Pearl.

When Judy approached, Mrs Crawford said, 'Nice to see you again, love.' She glanced meaningfully at Granny. 'Granny here insisted on coming. She asked Mr Teevan to bring us in his car—'

'I'm afraid she's a bit ancient,' said Mr Teevan, smiling. Noticing Granny's glare, he added hastily, 'The car, I mean.' Reddening, he stammered, 'What I mean is, we vets may get a special petrol ration, but it doesn't stretch to new springs for the car.'

Fortunately, Peewee came skipping over, and Granny beamed at him. 'You show 'em, Peewee,' she told him. 'You and Wee Billy.'

Then she glanced sharply at Judy. 'I remember you, the wean from Dublin.'

Judy grinned weakly. Granny went on, 'Would you believe, a wee girl playing football.' They waited for her criticism, but she went on, 'She's well able for them fellas.' She collapsed into a volley of coughs. When she could speak, she gazed around. 'So where *is* Billy?'

'He has to rally the team, Granny.' Peewee pointed to where Billy was deep in a huddle with the players.

'He's giving them a pep talk,' said Mrs Crawford.

'I think they're going to need it,' said Judy, as the whistle blew for the second half.

❖ ❖ ❖

The second half started slowly. Judy, shivering on the sideline, saw Karl jumping up and down to keep warm. The village team passed the ball up the field, and suddenly, a tall boy who had scored earlier was thundering towards the goal. All eyes were on the ball as it rose high in the air.

But this time Gaby was ready. He gave a phenomenal leap and, with a cry of triumph, knocked the ball wide with his outstretched hand. There was a roar of delight from the spectators.

Eva nudged Judy. 'Look at Yakobi,' she giggled. 'He's jumping up and down like a two-year-old!' He was. Even Mr Senesh had allowed himself a smile.

There wasn't long to go. 'They're going to win,' sighed Pearl. 'We haven't even got one goal.'

'It's not over yet,' said Eva.

'And I always thought football was boring,' said Judy.

'Quick, quick!' cried Pearl, grabbing her arm. Karl, in his dogged way, was nursing the ball along. He cleared it to Billy, who passed it out to Peewee, on the wing. Peewee raced up the pitch, outrunning the opponents bearing down on him.

'C'mon, Peewee!' shouted Wee Billy. He was echoed by spectators along the sidelines, and especially loudly, by Granny and Mrs Crawford.

Peewee ran like the wind. Danny, nearby, took the ball as Peewee was repeatedly challenged, then passed it back. Finally, at the vital moment, Peewee passed the ball to Grace. Beating the last defender, she whacked the ball, with all her strength, over the goalkeeper's head and into the back of the net.

Amid the cheers, Eva said to Judy, her eyes shining,

'Imagine – a girl scoring for our team!'

'Good old Grace!' shouted Pearl.

'They were all really good,' said Rina, enthusiastically. 'The whole team.'

As the final whistle blew, Judy added, 'But we couldn't have done it without Peewee, and Wee Billy.'

33

Where is Home?

A few days after the excitement of the match, Judy woke up to the realisation that it was her last week at Millisle. And ironically, the very next morning she was assigned to the hen-house once again.

This time, though, it was a very different experience. The work, which had once been so difficult and exhausting, now seemed routine, and she and Grace gossiped easily about the football match.

'It's funny,' said Judy, as she packed the eggs. 'Even though we lost, that one goal made it feel like a victory.'

'I heard a few people were hopping mad to see a girl playing,' said Grace. 'But maybe one day, women playing football won't be unusual.'

'It's a shame your brother couldn't see you score,' said Judy.

'I told him his shirt brought me luck,' grinned Grace, tipping a bucket of mash into the wheelbarrow. 'That Billy was a grand coach, all the same. He had everyone playing in the right positions.'

'Pity Eileen, his girlfriend, couldn't come to the match,' said Judy. 'Peewee told us that she has consumption – that's TB, same as my sister Tilly. But Peewee says she's getting better.'

'That's good,' said Grace.

As they pushed the heavy wheelbarrow outside, Grace pushed back her flaming hair. 'We had a queer mix of people in our team,' she said, 'but it worked out fine, all playing together.'

◆ ❖ ◆

At lunch-time, Grace, picking up one of the empty cartons in which the egg-boxes were packed, said to Judy, 'Come on, I've something to show you.'

Curious, Judy followed her across the yard to the shed beside the laundry, where there was a large basket in which everyone dumped their dirty washing. It was usually overflowing with wet, muddy work-clothes. There, nestling among the washing was the tabby Farm cat, with four tiny, mewing kittens.

Judy knelt down beside them. 'They're so sweet!' she said. She picked one up and cuddled its warm, squirming little body, then put it down hastily as the mother cat gave a yowl of complaint.

Behind them, Karl's voice said, 'Their eyes are just open.' He and Norman, on their way back from the workshop, had stopped to look. Karl bent his head over the box, close to Judy's, and they stroked the kittens together, the brown wing of his hair falling forward over his eyes. Judy felt an inexplicable glow at his presence – combined with irritation at Norman, who had launched into a lecture about the superiority of dogs over cats, even though no one was listening.

Grace said briskly, 'I'm afraid this family will have to move to another home.' With capable hands, she lifted the cat and kittens into the carton. 'I'll take them to the boiler shed. It's warm there.'

As they turned to go, Karl said to Judy, 'I've just heard. Rosa is coming tomorrow to the Farm.'

'That's great,' she said. 'Is she–'

She broke off as Karl gazed past her, in the direction of the boiler shed. He pointed, and Judy, turning, saw the mother cat picking her way back across the cobbles, her topaz eyes intent, carrying one of her kittens by the scruff of its neck. Leaping up on the washing-basket, she deposited the kitten back on the clothes, repeating the task until she had all four kittens back where she wanted them.

A few minutes later Grace, heaving an exaggerated sigh, appeared with the box.

Judy and Norman started to laugh, but Karl said urgently, 'Can we not leave them there?'

They stared at him.

'After all,' he said simply, 'for them, it is their home.'

After a moment Grace nodded and took away the box, leaving the cat sitting regally among its young.

Judy and Karl walked back to the dining-hall together, without words. Even Norman, Judy noticed, had the sense to keep his mouth shut.

34

Arrival and Departure

'Karli, Karli! I'm here!' Rosa's voice rang out as Mr Freeman carefully lifted her out of the car and handed her a pair of crutches. Her leg and foot were still encased in plaster, but she was laughing with delight as Karl hurried over to her.

Judy was changing sheets in the dormitory with Susi when Karl and Mr Freeman staggered in, carrying several suitcases sent with Rosa. These turned out to be full of pretty, but totally unsuitable, clothes, plus a stack of toys.

'These should keep Rosa happy,' said Mr Freeman, heaving them on to the bed. He added quietly, to Karl, 'The Goulds were sad to see her go, but Mr Gould told me that perhaps it was for the best.'

As he left, Mr Freeman asked him, 'Any luck with those refugee organisations?'

Karl explained that he was still waiting for a reply from his cousin in America.

'I hope it works out,' said Mr Freeman. 'I wish there was more we could all do.'

That night, Judy helped Rosa get ready for bed. Snug in her pyjamas, she looked through the heap of toys sent by the Goulds and selected a ragged doll, clearly worn from long use.

'Is this the "real" doll from home, Rosa – the one you told me about?' asked Judy.

'Yes,' she answered. 'This is Mitzi. The other one is sick.' Judy knew what had happened, but saying nothing. She tucked the doll in beside Rosa and asked if she would like a bedtime story. Rosa nodded and handed Judy a tattered storybook with a picture of a dog on the cover. When Judy explained that she couldn't read German, Rosa said, 'It's all right, Judy.' And she proceeded to read it aloud, in German, to Judy, though she obviously knew it by heart.

Peering at the book over Rosa's shoulder, Judy was struck by how much the dog in the book looked like the one she had seen in Karl's photos of Vienna. Sadness stole over her as she recalled Karl telling her what had happened to their dog, and warning her not to tell Rosa.

Careful to hide her emotion, Judy bent to kiss the child good night, and crept away.

◆ ❖ ◆

On her last working day, Judy screwed up her courage to go to the byre with Karl for the evening milking, so that, when she was back in Dublin, she could at least tell everyone she had milked a cow. Luckily, there was no one around – apart from Rosa, still on her crutches – to watch or mock.

'You're quite sure that's not Alice?' Judy asked Karl suspiciously, indicating the cow.

'No,' he grinned. 'It's Daisy.' Judy wasn't sure, but she hoped he was right.

Karl sat on the three-legged stool beside the cow and effortlessly, rhythmically squeezed its swollen udders, directing a stream of warm, sweet-smelling milk into the bucket. He leant his head against the cow's sleek flank, murmuring to her soothingly.

Rosa watched with interest. 'Karli,' she said eventually, 'how did all that milk get into the cow?'

Karl and Judy suppressed their laughter, and Karl gave Rosa a halting explanation in German. She nodded uncertainly.

Then Judy took over, reaching gingerly for the cow. Streams of milk went in all directions, and the cow flicked its tail and shifted its heavy hindquarters. The stool overbalanced, and Judy fell with a thump onto the hay-strewn floor of the byre. Rosa giggled, and Karl grinned as he put out a hand and pulled Judy to her feet.

'All right, Judy?'

She found herself standing close to him, surprised by a kind of warmth that she faintly remembered from the long-ago time when she had stood for a few seconds in Karl's arms. His face was so near, she could feel his breath on her cheek. His grey-green eyes looked into hers. Even though Rosa was there, would he put his arm around her? Would he say how he felt about her?

For a few seconds they stood together in the dim, steamy byre.

Then Rosa's plaintive voice said, 'Karli, Judy, the cow is waiting.'

The spell was broken. The moment had passed. Karl drew away abruptly, and the milking lesson ended.

Judy sighed to herself. She liked Karl so much, and now that she was leaving, probably nothing would ever happen; he would never say anything, to bring them closer.

◆ ❖ ◆

Everyone gathered to see the Dublin crowd off. Even Gaby came by to give them a cool nod and mutter, 'Good luck.' Eva, Susi and, surprisingly, Rina kissed Pearl and Judy on both cheeks.

'We'll miss you on the team,' Danny told Norman, with a grin. 'Have a good journey.' Grace handed Judy a bag of new-laid eggs, still warm, and Mr Senesh appeared to thank them personally for their help on the Farm.

Yakobi shook their hands and gave them apples from the orchard. He murmured to Judy, 'You have grown up this summer, I think, my dear Judy.' He cocked his head, like an inquisitive mole. 'Millisle was not so bad in the end, yes?'

Judy smiled absently, searching for Karl. She'd barely seen him since the milking lesson. Surely he would come to say goodbye?

At the last minute, as they were carrying out their cases, Karl appeared, holding Rosa by the hand. Since coming to Millisle, Rosa had looked healthier and happier every day. Just that morning, she had finally been allowed to discard her crutches. She reached up and wound her arms around Judy's neck, murmuring, 'I don't want you to go, Judy.'

As Judy straightened up, Karl looked directly at her. 'I

hope, Judy, you will come back to Millisle.'

Her heart jumped. Back to Millisle ... It almost sounded like an invitation. But did he mean it, or was he just being his usual polite self? After all, the barrier was still between them; Vienna, and Lisl, still cast their long shadows.

They were already in the bus when Pearl, who had been gazing out of the window at Danny, suddenly said, 'Judy, someone wants you!'

Peewee was running up the road, waving and gesticulating, a cow ambling behind him. Judy opened the bus window, and he shouted, 'Hey, Judy, I brought Alice to say g'bye to you!'

Judy called, 'Thanks, Peewee!'

'And Granny says you've to come for another visit,' he called. 'She wants to tell you more about her mill days. She said, "That wean has a bit of spirit!"'

Brushing his sandy hair out of his eyes, he grinned, and the bus pulled away.

35

Afterwards

The next day, after the Saturday-morning service, the refugees came out of the Farm's makeshift synagogue to a breezy, sunlit day. As it was the Sabbath, Karl had no Farm job to do, so he decided to take Rosa to the orchard.

He lay back in the lush, damp grass, splashed with golden dandelions. His grandfather's prayer shawl, in its velvet bag, rested beside him. High in the blue above, skeins of geese were flying south towards Strangford Lough. Rosa gathered handfuls of daisies and started making a daisy chain.

She's happy here, thought Karl. Her ankle's better; she's stopped sleepwalking. So why did he feel sad?

The previous day, he had at last got a reply from their American cousin. She explained that she had moved to Canada, and that his parents' earlier letters and his own more recent one, had only recently reached her. She offered to send money to the aid organisation Karl had contacted, to help purchase visas so that his family could escape from Vienna.

He should have been full of joy and relief. But he wasn't.

'Karl,' Rosa asked plaintively, 'why has Judy gone? She was fun.'

Was that why he felt sad? Because they had gone, the Dublin crowd – and Judy? He had backed off from getting too close to her. She had wanted to know about him and Lisl, and he hadn't been ready to share that story.

Resolutely he rose to his feet, trying to switch his thoughts to something else. He and Danny and the others were going to the beach after lunch, to rent a fishing-boat; they would row out, not far from the shore, and maybe catch a few silvery fish, and throw them back.

But he couldn't get Judy out of his mind – her liveliness, her sharpness, her unexpected sympathy. And the memory of that strange moment in the cow byre, when he had drawn back. Back from what?

Would she come back to the Farm? Maybe he should speak to Mr Senesh and, if he agreed, write and ask if she could come next Easter. With luck, his parents and Oma could be safely out of Austria by then, and he might be able to forget the past – Vienna, the Nazis, and Lisl – and really get to know Judy.

Was that possible?

PART FOUR

Liebe Judy!
Judy and Karl's Letters:
Dublin & Millisle,
Winter 1940

36

Millisle Settlement Farm
County Down
Northern Ireland
25 September 1940

Liebe Judy!

You will be surprised to get a letter from me. I got your address from Mr Senesh. Here in Millisle we miss your group very much. I've asked Mr Senesh if you could come back to help us at Easter. He agrees, but will your parents give permission? I hope you want to come. Not just for the work. It's not the same since you left.

Last night we heard on the news that many cities in England were bombed by the Luftwaffe (the Nazi German air force). London is bombed every night – it's called the Blitz – and people have to sleep in shelters or in the Underground. Grace's sister is in the Women's Auxiliary Air Force, and Peewee's uncle is at sea with convoys, so they are both in danger. Only here, and in Dublin too, are people safe from bombs. We're lucky.

Rosa is happy here. Her ankle is better, and she's been helping with the harvest. Grace calls her 'my little chickadee'; it's from a film. In a few weeks we'll have potato holidays from school, and Peewee is coming to help us dig the potatoes. He's told me to say he is asking for you.

Please write. It's nice to get letters.

Your friend,
Karl Muller

PS. Yesterday, because it was the New Year, after the synagogue we had apples and honey for a sweet year. We all prayed to see our families again. That would be sweet. It's a year and a half since I saw mine, and I've had no message for months. But my American cousin has sent money, which the refugee organisation will try to get to Vienna. So maybe they'll soon be free!

❖

98 Stamer Street,
Portobello,
Dublin
10 October 1940

Dear Karl,

I was so happy to get your letter! At breakfast, everyone was staring at it, but there was no Postilion to tell them what was in it!!

I would love to come back to the Farm. I'm waiting till Ma and Da are in a good mood to ask them, but they're very worried about my sister Tilly. She's back in the sanatorium. We visited her there. She's so thin and white, and her eyes look enormous, like the poor little foal. I couldn't go too near her, but I read the Evening Mail to her from across the room.

The Farm seems so far away now, like a dream. I often think about you (I mean all of you, of course) – even about the hens, and Alice, and the match, of course! Here it's boring, and mostly you'd hardly know there was a war. There's no proper blackout. There are no sweet coupons, no tanks or troop carriers on the roads, no soldiers in uniform.

Nora's sister has gone to work in a munitions factory in England, and Norman's brother has joined the British army. In Dublin everyone goes around on bikes because of the fuel shortage, and my brother Michael took a girl to a college hop (that's a dance) in a horse-drawn cab!!

I'm glad Rosa is fine. How are Eva and Rina and the others? I hope I can get back to Millisle. I don't know about Pearl or Norman, but if my parents let me, I'll come, even on my own.

Write soon.

Your good friend,
Judy

PS. I think this must be the longest letter I've ever written!!!

❖

Millisle Settlement Farm
County Down
5 January 1941

Liebe Judy! (That is how you start a letter in German.)

I got your letter, and I hope very much you can come back here, even if the others cannot.

I have lots of schoolwork, and most of us are attending night courses, too. I've also joined the ATC and I'll be learning to fly gliders. I met Wee Billy at Newtownards Airfield, and he promised to bring Eileen to the Farm as soon as she's well enough, maybe in the spring.

My cousin Tommy sent me very bad news he heard, about my old headmaster in Vienna, Herr Klaar, who was always kind to me. He was caught sheltering people from the Nazis, and he was taken to prison and shot. I was very sad to hear this. He was so brave, and so is our neighbour, Leni, who helps my family. Most people don't risk opposing the Nazis, like a girl I knew. I thought she was my friend, but she rejected me and ended our friendship because I'm Jewish. It's hard to forget this. Her name was Lisl. I haven't told any-one before, but it's easier in a letter.

The weather is very cold now, and the cobbles in the yard are slippery with ice. The farm is beautiful in the snow, but the ground is like a rock, and it's no fun trying to pull up frozen Brussels sprouts and turnips.

Mrs Crawford asked me and Rosa to tea. There was a Christmas tree, which Rosa thought very pretty. I explained that we Jews do not have this, and Granny and Peewee were surprised! Mrs Crawford is knitting a pixie hood to keep

Rosa's ears warm. Granny told Rosa about the linen mill, but I'm afraid Rosa couldn't understand much. Granny asked also for 'that wain from Dublin'!

Eva and Danny are here in the rec, and they say hello. Danny's writing to Pearl. Rina has just come back from her Red Cross course, and she says to tell you that you were not the worst. From Rina, that's praise! But we know her bark is worse than her bite. (I remember that's what Mrs Crawford said about Granny, and I didn't know then what she meant, but now I do!)

From your friend,
Karl

PS Danny and I have finished off the Spitfire. Now we're making a model Sunderland flying boat. The real ones are made in Belfast.

❖

Portobello
Dublin
18 February 1941

Dear Karl,

I had to write straight away to tell you this. At dinner, Ma said the news from the sanatorium was good. Tilly is having a remission (that means she's a bit better for now) and she might be able to come home in April, for the Passover festival. Then Da muttered, 'What about the child?' (I ask you – child!!)

Well, I barged in quickly and said I wanted to go back to help on the Farm, and it would be nice to be there for Passover. It'll be the Easter holidays, so I wouldn't miss any school, and they wouldn't have to worry about me catching Tilly's TB.

Da said he was pleased I wanted to help. Michael muttered, 'That'll be the day,' under his breath, but I ignored him.

So I might be able to come back to Millisle in a few weeks!! Pearl can't come; her mother is sick. But Norman hopes to, and he's going to bring his bike on the train. I can't wait to see you again – and all the others, of course.

Yours ever,
Judy

PS That was sad, what you wrote about Lisl. I hope some day you won't be so unhappy about her any more.

PPS I like when you write 'Liebe Judy!' It's sort of romantic.

❖

Millisle Settlement Farm
County Down
7 April 1941

Dear Judy,

I know you are coming next week, but I am writing to tell you that Karl has had bad news from home and he is very upset. He will not tell us what is wrong. He only says he wants to leave the Farm. Even Yakobi cannot find out Karl's trouble. He hardly speaks, even to Rosa. I hope when you come you can help him. I have never seen him like this.

We will all be pleased to see you, Judy.

Your friend,
Eva

PART FIVE

Blitz!
Karl, Judy & Peewee:
Millisle, Easter 1941

37

Bad News

In spite of the warning letter from Eva, Judy had half-hoped Karl would be at Donaghadee to meet the train. Over the months of their separation, she had thought a great deal about him and Rosa, and had talked about him endlessly to a long-suffering Nora. Memories of certain incidents from their time together had haunted her – the 'bull' episode, looking at the photos with Rosa, the milking lesson ...

When she left the Farm, Judy had felt that the future for her and Karl – and whether he had any special feelings for her – was doubtful. But Karl's letters, and some of the confidences in them, had seemed to her to bring them much closer, and she longed to see him again.

Instead, Yakobi, with his sweet welcoming smile, was there to meet her and Norman. Judy tried not to show her disappointment as they loaded their luggage and Norman's bike into the farm cart.

'Where's Karl?' Judy asked Yakobi, when they were seated in the cart and Molly's hooves were clopping rhythmically along the Millisle road. Yakobi shrugged sadly. 'I haven't seen him all day,' he said. 'He is very upset, but he cannot talk about what is troubling him.'

'But aren't his family getting visas to escape from Vienna?' asked Judy.

Yakobi shook his head. 'I know he was trying to get money to them for that,' he said. 'But if they had got out, we would have heard.'

On the train from Dublin, while Norman was devouring a series of detective stories which he produced from the bottomless pocket of his familiar hairy jacket, Judy had read and re-read the letter from Eva, and all of Karl's letters, searching for a clue. What had happened? Obviously it was something to do with his family – or maybe to do with Lisl? But when Karl had been worried before, he had always hidden it, put on a front, kept smiling. What had changed him?

◆ ❖ ◆

At the Farm everyone was busy, though several people stopped briefly to welcome them. Rosa came running up, thinner and taller, her sausage curls transformed into a golden mop. She was cuddling one of the kittens, now a plump tabby like its mother. 'Judy, Judy!' she cried. 'Will you read me a story tonight?'

'You're too grown-up for that,' teased Judy, stroking the kitten.

Then Danny appeared, with Eva. They were both smiling, and to Judy they looked somehow older.

'It's good to have you back,' said Danny. He added, to Judy, 'Pity Pearl couldn't come.'

'Hi, Danny, Eva,' said Norman. 'Why is everyone rushing around like headless chickens?'

'Passover's only two days away!' said Eva. 'We're all busy with spring cleaning, and cooking, and preparing the special food for the Seder.' As Danny helped Norman with his suitcase and bike, she drew Judy aside. 'You got my letter?'

Judy nodded. 'Have you found out any more?'

Eva shook her head. 'Grace tried to talk to Karl, but it was no use. He's so angry and unhappy.'

'D'you know where he is?'

'I saw him this morning, walking up towards the village,' said Eva. 'He's probably gone to the windmill. He often goes there.'

'I'll just dump my stuff,' said Judy. 'Then I'll follow him.'

Eva glanced at her fondly. 'I'm so glad you're here, Judy. Karl talked a lot about you, before this happened. I'm sure you'll be able to help him.'

'I hope so,' said Judy uncertainly. She understood all about feeling angry and unhappy, but only because of smaller things, not the sort of problems that Karl had to deal with. And if he wouldn't talk to Eva or Yakobi or Grace, why should he talk to her?

◆ ❖ ◆

Karl, sitting high on the tiny wooden gallery beside the fantail at the back of the windmill, sprang to his feet when he saw Judy at the foot of the building. She was wearing a new jacket and skirt, and her hair, windblown in the breeze, was gathered back the way he liked.

Reaching the top of the ladder, she saw, in the second before he summoned a faint smile, that his face was clenched in misery. She sat down beside him and they gazed out over the peaceful scene – the farms spread out below, the trees and hedgerows clothed in fresh new leaves, the roofs of the village, and the distant, sparkling sea.

Judy broke the stillness. 'What's wrong, Karl?'

He turned to her, his grey-green eyes filled with tears. A remembered phrase shot into her mind, "The world's more full of weeping ..."

Hesitantly, she laid her hand gently on Karl's. He did not remove his. For a few moments, neither of them spoke.

Then he said slowly, 'It's hard to talk about it.'

'But Karl, surely whatever it is, it's better to talk about it.'

After another long moment he nodded, as though coming to a decision. He said in a rush, 'I feel so guilty, Judy. So bad that I haven't been able to tell anyone. It's like when I couldn't talk about Lisl.'

Judy waited, her hand still on his. With an effort, he continued. 'My parents saved Rosa and me – they sent us away from danger. But I've failed them. They've been deported – maybe to a prison camp, maybe even to a dreadful place like Dachau, where my uncle Rudi was.'

'Deported?' repeated Judy, horrified. 'How did you hear?'

'Their neighbour, Leni, smuggled a note out to my cousin Tommy. My mother slipped it to her before they were forced into the trucks.' He unfolded a torn scrap of paper, with a few words in German scrawled on it. 'It just says, *Tell Karl we all have to go east, together with Tommy's family and little Benji. God bless and keep him and Rosa.'*

'But the money from America that you wrote about–'

'It was no good,' he said bleakly. 'The refugee organisation wrote to me that my parents did have a chance to get visas to go to Hong Kong. But because Oma, my grandmother, is old and sick, they weren't allowed to bring her, and they refused to go without her.'

'But Karl,' said Judy desperately, 'there's still hope. You told me before that no one knows for sure where people are deported to. Maybe it won't be a prison.'

Karl was silent.

'Anyway,' Judy went on, 'you shouldn't feel guilty. You did your best to help them. They would know that.'

Karl looked away. 'It wasn't enough,' he said in strangled tones. 'And now I can't just stay here in Millisle, doing nothing. I've had enough of waiting for things to happen to me.' He sounded angry, almost hysterical. 'I've decided to run away, tomorrow night, after the Passover meal. I'm going to England. With my ATC training, if I lie about my age, I might get into the Air Force. Then I can help to stop the Nazis and what they're doing.'

This was a different Karl, thought Judy – a Karl of whom she had only caught occasional glimpses before.

A harsh, melancholy sound made them both look up. Hazy strings of birds flew over them in groups, calling to each other, their powerful white-flashed wings beating slowly.

'Those are Brent geese,' said Karl. 'They always leave when spring comes. Mr Armstrong told me they go north to the Arctic to breed.' He paused. 'I saw them flying in, the day after you left.'

As they watched the flight, Karl said bitterly, 'These birds, they can fly together, right over countries and borders. It doesn't matter to them what is happening to people below.'

There was a silence.

Judy sprang up. 'Karl, let's go back to the Farm,' she said. 'Rosa will be waiting. On the way we can talk about what you should do. Maybe I can help.'

She took his hand, and together they descended the ladder.

38

The Plan

Late that night in the chilly dormitory, with everyone asleep around them, Judy repeated Karl's news to Eva.

'I've heard before about these deportations,' Eva said. 'We are all so worried, because most of us don't know if this has happened to our families.' She sighed, and went on, 'But for Karl to run away from the Farm doesn't make sense. What's the point of it? And what about Rosa?'

'I said that to him,' said Judy. 'He says Rosa is happy and safe here, but he has to go. He's even asked Peewee to help him get to the ferry!'

'Didn't Peewee try to talk him out of it?'

'Karl said Peewee asked no questions, just said he'd help, because Karl is his friend.'

'There will be trouble,' said Eva. 'Refugees aren't supposed to travel without a police permit, and we have to say where we're going, and why.' She paused, thinking. 'Should we talk to Yakobi?'

Judy shook her head. 'Karl made me promise not to. Anyway, I don't think even Yakobi can help. Karl's set on leaving Millisle. He said there's no way he'll change his mind.' She slipped on her pyjamas, over her underwear. 'All I could do was try to persuade him to go to Dublin instead, and maybe go on to England from there. I told him there'd be less chance of being caught and sent back.'

Eva frowned. 'You know, it will affect all of us. Mr Senesh, and Rina and Gaby and the others will be furious.' She paused. 'And why is it any better if Karl goes first to Dublin?'

Judy crawled into the cold bed with a shiver. 'If he agrees to go to Dublin, Eva, I told him I'd go with him.'

Eva stared at her. Judy went on, 'Maybe when we're there – away from Millisle, away from the war – he'll see how crazy all this is, that it won't help.' She murmured, half to herself, 'Anyway, I have to help Karl. I don't want to let him down.' She added silently, Like Lisl did.

◆ ❖ ◆

Karl drifted in and out of a restless sleep. Wandering through his dreams, the figures of his parents were shadowy and indistinct, their faces ghost-pale, always turned away from him. When he woke, Karl was overwhelmed with panic at the future that lay ahead for him, a blank screen with no guidance, no certainties.

Since the news about his family, he had begun to realise that he had to make a future for himself and for Rosa, in case their parents did not survive the war. Leaving

Millisle now, he had told himself, going to fight – at least he would be doing something. And it would put off, for the present, this bleak, frightening, lonely future that yawned in his mind.

The main problem, Karl knew, was Rosa. But his over-taxed mind refused to deal with her. He would leave her a letter, explaining why he had left and telling her to wait for him on the Farm and not worry about him. When he returned, he would take care of her.

He also refused to consider the effect his running away would have on the other refugees' position. For once, he told himself, he wasn't going to think about consequences. Nor was he going to think about how much he was depending on Judy's support, and on the reluctant loyalty of Danny and Eva, and on Peewee's unhesitating trust.

The plan was for Karl and Judy to slip away after the Passover meal, during the traditional prayers and songs, which would continue into the night. Karl would borrow the battered Farm bike, and Norman, sworn to secrecy, had agreed to lend Judy the bike he had brought from Dublin. Peewee, on his own bike, would lead them across country to Lisburn, about twenty-five miles away. They would leave the bikes there, for Peewee to bring back to the Farm later, and Karl and Judy would catch the early-morning train to Dublin.

After that, everything became uncertain. When they reached Dublin, Judy had said, she would bring Karl to her house. But she had warned him that she wasn't sure how her parents would react, because of Tilly's illness and espe-cially when they discovered that Karl had left the Farm illegally. But eventually, somehow, he would cross to England and attempt to join the Forces.

It was hard to think that far ahead. As Karl tossed and twisted, dark, ominous thoughts circled like predators, until outside, the first birds began to chirrup their melodious dawn chorus.

39

Running Away

Judy glanced around the crowded dining-hall, at the tables gleaming with white cloths and shining glasses and platters of matzah, a sort of cracker eaten on Passover. The familiar story of the Exodus was recited, glasses of wine were sipped, and special foods were passed around, all to remind them of the Jewish people's miraculous deliverance from slavery in ancient times.

Apart from a few guests, some in uniform, Judy now knew most of the faces. She remembered how homesick she had felt the summer before, on her first Friday evening at the Farm. Now, of course, she realised that, whatever she felt, the refugees' homesickness was much deeper, especially at times of family celebration like this – Danny, who hadn't heard from his family in Berlin for over a year; Rina and Susi, who hadn't even been allowed to say goodbye to their imprisoned parents; Eva, whose bedside locker bore photos of her parents, grandparents and baby brother; Karl, Gaby, the little boy who always cried; and all the others.

As the meal began, people chatted; some tried to smile and be happy, others discussed the gloomy war news – battles in North Africa, the fall of Greece to the Nazis, the nightly bombing of British cities, and the remote hope that America might enter the war and tip the balance against the Nazis.

Yakobi came over to their table and spoke gently to Karl. Judy knew that Karl must be gripped by guilt, as she was herself, at deceiving Yakobi. But in his new forceful way, Karl had explained that if Yakobi suspected their plan, he would be obliged to tell Mr Senesh, so they couldn't risk it.

When Yakobi moved on, Judy's eyes met Karl's. Only an hour to go. Her stomach tightened with nervous anticipation.

◆ ❖ ◆

In the flurry as everyone cleared away the meal, Judy and Karl slipped away to their dormitories. They changed into dark clothes and packed small knapsacks with necessities. At the last moment, Karl added his grandfather's old prayer shawl, which he had used faithfully at Saturday services. He left Oma's iron ring, carefully wrapped, for Rosa.

Soon they were on their bikes and under way, Judy struggling with the unfamiliar, heavy boy's bike. It had been a dull, overcast day, but the sky cleared as they rode into Millisle. It was Easter Tuesday, still part of the holiday weekend, and the village was quiet. From the laneway beside Crawford's pub, a sweet, high whistle sounded, and Judy's heart lifted at the sight of Peewee's welcoming grin through the gathering dusk.

Greeting them, he said, 'Will you be missed at the Farm, d'you think?'

'Not tonight,' said Karl. 'There is so much coming and going, and many people around. If anyone asks, Danny or Eva or Norman will make some excuse.'

Judy suppressed thoughts of the next day, when their absence was bound to be noticed.

Grateful for the moon lighting their way, they sped along empty roads, through blacked-out farms and villages, breathing hard, speaking little, mechanically following Peewee's dim rear light. Once, a white horse, ghostly in the gloom, cantered up to the hedge to watch them pass.

Don't think, just keep pedalling, Judy told herself. There's no going back now.

◆ ❖ ◆

At Newtownards, they skirted the main street, in case anyone should recognise them, and carried on through the Craigantlet Hills towards Dundonald, the looming mass of Scrabo Hill and its tower behind them. The road was uphill, and Judy was getting tired and hungry. After a while she slowed down and called to Peewee to stop.

Karl came up behind her and dismounted. 'What's wrong?'

'Can we have a rest?' said Judy. 'I'm not used to this bike.'

Peewee had turned and ridden back to them. 'We can stop ahead, beside Cregagh church,' he said. 'It's sheltered from the wind.'

Only the forlorn barking of a dog broke the deep, intense

silence of the night. They leant their bikes against the wall and squatted on the grassy slope, gazing out over Belfast and its gantries floating below them in the pale moonlight, and in the distance, the dark, glistening waters of Belfast Lough.

Karl was preoccupied. Judy, wearily massaging her aching legs, asked herself gloomily, Why am I doing this? It's for Karl, but does he really care if I'm here or not?

Peewee remained cheerful. Delving into his rucksack, he produced a thermos flask and a paper bag.

'Peewee, you're a wonder,' said Karl, a trace of his old self reappearing, as they gulped down the hot, reviving tea.

'I only brought apples,' said Judy.

Peewee unwrapped thick hunks of wholemeal bread. 'Made the sandwiches myself,' he said proudly. Offering one to Karl, he added, 'Don't worry, there's no ham. It's cheese, from the farm.'

As they munched, Karl made an effort to chat. 'Is Wee Billy still on guard duty at Newtownards?' he asked Peewee.

'Aye. He's back at the airfield. Him and me went to a match today at Linfield – it was great. Not as good as ours, though.' He grinned.

'How's his girlfriend?' asked Judy, between mouthfuls.

Peewee hesitated. 'I think she's a bit better. Billy wants them to get married. But everyone says they're too young. There was a bit of a row–'

He was interrupted by the piercing wail of a siren.

'Air-raid warning!' said Karl, as they scrambled to their feet.

'It's probably nothing,' said Peewee. 'Still, I suppose we'd better wait for the all-clear.' Fastening his rucksack, he added, 'Funny though, my ma said she'd seen a German plane flying low towards the city, yesterday. Billy said–'

'Shhh,' said Judy. 'What's that?'

They could hear a low, growling hum, growing louder, swelling to a roar. Karl stiffened. 'It sounds like planes, many planes.'

'Look!' shouted Peewee. From the direction of Belfast Lough, they could see rows of bombers flying in formation, sweeping towards the city, filling the sky with thunder, until the air all around them seemed to vibrate.

Karl grabbed Judy and Peewee, and they flung themselves on the ground, huddling close to the stone wall of the little church. One plane flew so low that they could see the swastika marking on the tail and the figure of the pilot inside.

Karl put his mouth to Judy's ear. She could feel his warm breath, and the comfort of his arm encircling her. 'Like Yakobi said,' he whispered, as the sound above grew deafening, 'the war has come to Northern Ireland.'

So much for all the people who said it would never happen, thought Judy. Her hand to her mouth, she looked down at the defenceless, sleeping city, with the bombers inexorably approaching.

'Poor Belfast,' she whispered.

40

Blitz on Belfast

For the rest of their lives, the next few hours would remain indelibly printed on all their minds.

Before their eyes, hundreds of small white silk parachutes floated down, carrying flares that cast a ghostly silver glow over the city, as bright as daylight. Added to the drone of the bombers, they heard the stutter of anti-aircraft guns from the Castlereagh Hills close to them.

'What are those?' whispered Judy, as the air filled with crackling sparks which burst into tiny flames as they reached the ground far below.

'They're like fireworks,' said Peewee.

'Not fireworks,' said Karl. 'Incendiary bombs.'

Slowly, gradually, the sparks of fire below spread, joined, and grew into a network of flame. Then they heard the deafening crump and shriek of heavy explosives hurtling down. Above, steadily, almost monotonously, the drone of yet more bombers continued.

In a short time, the city of Belfast – its streets, its houses and buildings, its shipyards and factories and mills, and its people – had become a huge lake of angry crimson and orange flame.

Peewee said something which Karl, in an unbelieving daze, could not hear. He shook his head, and Peewee pointed upwards, to where the sky over the city had turned a strange, dull red. Like the sky on Kristallnacht, thought Karl, when the synagogues were burning.

For what seemed like hours, the planes came in waves. Was anyone going to be left alive after this? Karl knew about the aerial bombing of towns and cities, from radio reports, newspapers, and cinema newsreels. Now, displayed below them, and ringing in their ears, was the fearsome reality.

'D'you see that cloud of thick black smoke?' said Judy.

'That's the shipyard,' said Peewee slowly. 'Harland and Wolff.'

Karl remembered his first journey to Millisle, and Mr Senesh pointing out the shipyard. For the first time that evening, his thoughts turned to the Farm, to Rosa and the others.

'Do you think they're all right at the Farm?' he asked Peewee.

'Belfast's the target,' replied Peewee, in a subdued tone. 'Millisle's twenty miles away.' He added bleakly, 'But I've got pals in the Shankill. Though I s'pose most people are safe in the air-raid shelters. And there must be bomb wardens and air-raid precaution, and firemen, and ...' His voice trailed off as they stared down at the burning city.

'How can firemen deal with that?' said Karl. 'Surely you'd need an incredible amount of water to put out all those fires.

And with bombs falling all around—'

'And buildings collapsing,' said Judy.

No one said, 'And the dead and injured.' But it was in all their minds.

They rose, stiff, deafened, and chilled to the bone. 'There's nothing we can do,' said Peewee bleakly. 'Better get on.'

◆ ❖ ◆

Back on the road, they turned south towards Lisburn. Traffic was appearing – bikes, horse-drawn vehicles, some piled with belongings, a few cars. People from the medical and fire services rushing into Belfast to help, thought Karl, and others hastening out of the city to escape the raid.

As he pedalled, a worm of unease about what he was doing began to stir inside Karl. What they had witnessed somehow put a different perspective on things. Was it right to be running away – wrapped up in his own private misery, abandoning Rosa and the others, dragging Judy and Peewee with him on this unreal journey – when these disastrous events were taking place all round them? The more he tried to suppress them, the stronger the doubts grew.

They pressed on, crossing the River Lagan, and eventually, just before Lisburn, the travellers reached the Belfast-Dublin road.

41

The Dublin Fire Brigades

Weary, silent and drained, the three stood at the roadside. Only a fitful moon and the blood-red glow in the sky lighted the darkness.

In the last hour of their ride, they had seen family groups with pitiful bundles, shocked and dazed, making their way on foot into the open country – many, it seemed, to sleep in ditches and under hedges. It was now the early hours of Wednesday, and cars and trucks, buses and bikes, every kind of conveyance, flowed past them, with masked headlights, leaving Belfast and heading towards Dublin. The roadside was crowded with pedestrians, some trying to hitch lifts.

Judy and Peewee, dirty and tired, had propped their bikes against a hedge and were squatting on the grass. Karl, numbed by the events of the night and the effort of their journey, knew the time had come to make up his mind about the doubts bubbling in his mind. But as he turned to Judy and Peewee, a bomb warden approached, waving everyone back from the road.

A procession of fire engines sped past them, unmasked headlights blazing, towards the burning city. They counted thirteen in all. Those on the roadside, including Karl, Judy and Peewee, waved and cheered as they passed, and the uniformed firemen on the tenders waved back and grinned. Then they were gone.

'Are they from Dublin?' asked Peewee.

The warden, his haggard face streaked with grime, heard him. 'Aye,' he said wearily. 'We've been sent out here to direct them through. The fires in Belfast are out of control.'

'But the South is neutral,' said Judy.

The warden removed his helmet with an exhausted movement. 'That may be,' he said. 'But help was asked of a neighbour, and help has been given.'

◆ ❖ ◆

'I don't know how to say this,' said Karl. 'But I – we have to go back. To Millisle.'

Judy and Peewee stared at him.

'I know I dragged you here, through this awful night,' he went on. 'I must have been mad. I think I had a sort of brainstorm because of the news about my family.' He wiped his forehead with a grubby handkerchief. 'Maybe I had to get away from Millisle to find out what I should have known, what the raid has told me. Until I can join up, my place is on the Farm, with Rosa, with you–' He looked at Judy with his old gentle look, '– with the others, and everyone who's helping us to work the Farm.'

Judy and Peewee exchanged glances. Then Judy touched

Karl's shoulder. 'Well, I s'pose, Karl,' she said wryly, 'in a way, there's no need, any more, for you to go and find the war. The war has come to us.'

They stood for a moment, linked by the light touch of her hand.

Peewee gave a colossal yawn. 'Don't know about you lot, but I'm dead on my feet,' he said. 'C'mon, on yer bikes.'

42

One More Death

The still-dark streets were empty when they toiled into Millisle village and turned into the yard beside Crawford's.

'I'll make us a bit of breakfast,' said Peewee. 'Not rashers, of course.' He grinned. 'There'll be no one about for a couple of hours yet. You can have a wee rest before you go back to the Farm.'

'Great,' said Judy. Stiffly, she clambered off the bike. 'I'm starving. And I'd like to sleep for a week.'

'With luck, they may not realise at the Farm that we were gone at all—' Karl was saying, as they entered the pub through the side door.

Peewee, in front, stopped dead. A light was on in the kitchen, and there was a murmur of voices and what sounded like someone crying.

Peewee frowned. 'Sounds like they're up. We're sure to be asked questions,' he muttered to the others. 'Sorry, but maybe you'd better go—'

He broke off as the kitchen door opened. Mrs Crawford

appeared, her face tear-stained and drained of colour, a shawl thrown round her shoulders. But what held their eyes, hypnotised them, was the apron she wore, so splattered with dirt and streaks of what looked like blood, that it was hard to tell it had once been white.

'Peewee!' she said, holding back tears. 'I was just going to see where you were.' She glanced at Judy and Karl. 'What—' she began.

Peewee, unable to take his eyes from her apron, said quickly, 'What's up, Mammy?'

She drew Peewee to her, and slow tears began to slide down her face.

Peewee's father appeared in the doorway. 'Ye'd better come in here, son,' he said heavily. 'There's bad news.'

'We should go,' Judy muttered to Karl. But as they turned to leave, Mrs Crawford stopped them.

'Please come in,' she whispered. 'You'll hear soon enough.'

Embarrassed at their intrusion, and aware that something was terribly wrong, Karl and Judy tiptoed into the kitchen. Mr Crawford stood rigidly behind Granny, who was slumped in her chair, staring ahead with unseeing eyes.

Mr Crawford was the only one able to speak. Grimly, quietly, he told them that Belfast was not the only place that had suffered a bombing raid that night. Incendiaries and high explosives had been dropped, not only on several other towns in the North, but also on Newtownards Airfield. The runways had been damaged, and there had been a direct hit on a Nissen hut, headquarters of the Young Soldiers' Battalion of the Inniskilling Fusiliers. Fifteen men had been wounded, and ten had been killed, including Wee Billy.

As they stood in a stunned silence, Mr Crawford gruffly went on to explain that his wife, as a former nurse, had hurried into Belfast to help, at the news of the raid. She had been on duty, first at the Mater Hospital and later at the Falls Road Public Baths, where the bodies of many of the dead had been brought and laid out for identification. As she was finally going off duty, after countless harrowing hours, she had heard of the Newtownards raid, but she had been unable to find out any details. She had hitched a lift and arrived home, just before an officer of the regiment called to the house to bring them word of the tragedy.

When Mr Crawford finished speaking, the room was filled with a deathly quiet, broken only by sobbing and the ticking of the clock over the fireplace. This can't have happened, thought Karl. Not to Billy, so brave and strong and determined – Billy, who could throw himself heart and soul into a children's football match, and understand the feelings of a group of unknown refugees. Glancing at Peewee's face, frozen in shock and misery, Karl told himself, now it's my turn to stand by him, to be his friend as he's been mine.

All this time, Granny had not moved. Mrs Crawford put an arm around her thin shoulders, and clasped Peewee to her with the other arm. Everyone stood with bowed heads while Mr Crawford recited a prayer.

After a while, he turned to Judy and Karl. 'I want to say,' he said haltingly, 'that although we are of different faiths, I hope–' He stopped, and his wife laid a hand on his shoulder. 'That is – would you be permitted to be with us at the funeral of our boy ...' His voice broke. After a moment, he went on hesitantly, 'We know he thought about you all at the Farm, and how you had to leave your families, because of the war–'

They could barely speak, from shock and sadness. But Karl cleared his throat and murmured, 'Of course we will come. Billy was our good friend–' He stopped.

Mrs Crawford, still weeping, said, 'Aye, wee loves, we know you cared for our Billy. And we must tell Eileen the news, poor wee girl, she's not so well–' Mechanically, she went to fill the kettle. 'There now, we'll have a cup of tea–'

Peewee said quietly, as he unhooked cups from the dresser, 'Was it very bad, Ma, in the city?'

His mother looked down at her filthy, bloodstained apron. 'It was terrible – terrible,' she repeated. 'Hundreds of people killed and injured. And we could do so little.' Her eyes were haunted. 'Everyone worked together to save people, to dig them out of the ruins with their bare hands, to bring them to hospitals, to treat them, to fight the fires ... In the shelters, they told us, people sang hymns together–'

'Poor souls, all of them,' whispered Granny, levering herself up from her chair.

She seemed feebler, as though she had shrunk even since the last time Karl had seen her. 'So many deaths this night,' she said hoarsely. 'I'm told our mill in York Street collapsed, on top of all the little houses around it, killing all the people.' She paused for a fit of coughing. 'It'll never be the same in Ulster – and it'll never be the same for us, without Wee Billy.'

Peewee brushed back the tears that sprang to his eyes. Karl stepped forward and put an arm round him.

Granny went on, 'Times have changed now, whether we like it or not.' Peering at Karl and Judy, silent observers of the scene, she added, 'Maybe we were divided here before. But there's all sorts around now, like these poor weans from foreign parts ... And we're all in the same war now.'

She sank back into her armchair, as if suddenly exhausted. 'All those deaths,' she murmured, 'but this is the one that hurts.'

43

The Road to Millisle

Dawn was just breaking, and the first birds were beginning to call, when Judy and Karl set out on the last lap of their journey.

Mrs Crawford, helped by Peewee and Judy, had made pot after pot of strong tea. Judy, sipping the tea, had felt her eyelids begin to droop with the weight of sadness and fatigue. Billy's death didn't seem real, but just another part of the endless, haunted night they had passed.

As she and Karl were about to leave for the Farm, they were all startled by a sharp rap on the door. Mr Crawford hurried out and returned almost immediately, moving slowly, like someone in a dream, or a nightmare. He was holding a small brown envelope.

Mrs Crawford's face had crumpled, and Granny's hand went to her mouth. 'The telegram,' she whispered. 'Now we know it's true.'

Neighbours began to call to offer condolences, and it was clear that word had begun to spread. Mr Crawford, grey and drawn, shook their hands, and left to send a message off to Billy's girlfriend. Mrs Crawford, her face wet with tears, kissed Judy and Karl goodbye.

Outside in the yard, Judy hugged Peewee. 'We'll always stay friends, Peewee,' she told him, 'won't we, Karl?'

Karl nodded. 'Of course.'

Peewee waved away their thanks and their words of sympathy. 'Mrs Adams from down the road, who just called in,' he told them, 'she said she'd heard that the Farm – and lots of other places round here – are filling up with people who've come from Belfast on account of the raid.' His voice shook. 'If only Billy had been on leave last night ... He had real bad luck. And the others, of course.' He was trying to speak normally. But they could see that something had gone out of Peewee – his chirpiness, his cheeriness, his sense of mischief.

Karl said quietly, 'It is hard to lose a brother.'

Judy guessed he was thinking not just about Billy, but also about Rosa. She herself felt a tremor of guilt about her own sister, about the way she had thought of Tilly's illness only as a nuisance, the reason she had been sent to Millisle. Now, after all that had happened, she felt differently about everything – Tilly, the Farm, the refugees, the war – almost as if she had shed an outer skin, like snakes do, and had emerged, not exactly transformed, but maybe changed for the better.

As they left, Peewee raised his hand in farewell. He lingered for a few moments. Then, shoulders drooping, he went slowly back inside.

Judy and Karl walked on, bone-weary, pushing their bikes because they were too tired to ride them. There was a stillness between them, a kind of ease.

'It seems a hundred years since we left the Farm,' said Judy. 'And as for everyone in Dublin – Nora, Pearl, Tilly, my ma and da – it feels as if they're on another planet.' She yawned. 'I'd better let them know I'm all right.'

Karl, too, felt as if he had lived years in the space of a single night. His mind was a haze of emotions – acute sorrow for Wee Billy, and for Peewee and the Crawfords; pity for all those others caught up in the terror of the air raid; relief at being almost back at the Farm and about to see Rosa – and something more complicated, something he couldn't define, towards Judy, trudging along beside him.

And as for his family, perhaps even now huddled in a train rumbling towards an unknown destination – he cared about them desperately. But he knew he had to let go the burning anger and bitterness that had possessed him. That didn't mean he would forget about his family – he would never stop thinking about them, and hoping that the war would end and they would be reunited. But meanwhile, he had to carry on trying to make a new life. That was what refugees had to do. And – as well as caring for Rosa – one of the first things he had to do in that new life, in this new country, was to help his friend Peewee through the dark times ahead.

'You know,' Karl said to Judy, 'when Yakobi came to me during the Passover meal, he told me that I must have hope. He said that without hope, we have nothing.'

She turned towards him. Wheeling his bike with one hand, Karl put his other arm awkwardly around her. She leant her head against his shoulder.

Linked together, they walked up the path that led to the Farm. The sun had risen, and the yard and the buildings, the meadows and fields and orchard, were all bathed in the pearly morning light. It blurred the hard edges, giving the Farm a luminous, dream-like quality, like a painting.

Then, with a cry of welcome, Rosa came running across the cobbles towards them.

AFTERWORD

Most of the events and places, and many of the characters in the story, are based on fact, although some details have been altered for the purposes of the story.

The Anschluss and the Kindertransports

The Anschluss, the annexation of Austria by Nazi Germany, took place on 12 March 1938. As Karl and his family observed in the story, the Nazis' triumphal march through Vienna was given an enthusiastic welcome by large crowds.

On that day, many Jews were abused, beaten and imprisoned like Karl's father and Uncle Rudi; very few were released. After the Anschluss, the lives of Austrian Jews changed almost overnight. Their homes and property were taken by the Nazis, and those who could, fled the country.

On 9 November 1938, Jewish synagogues, businesses and shops (like Karl's father's shoe shop) were burned and looted, and there were violent attacks on Jews, in towns and cities all over Germany and elsewhere. That night became known as 'Kristallnacht', the Night of Broken Glass. After that, most Jews redoubled their efforts to leave. But hardly any country, in Europe or elsewhere, including Ireland,

North or South, allowed refugees from the Nazis into their countries, in any numbers.

The Kindertransports were unique, in that about 10,000 unaccompanied children, from 3 months to 17 years of age, from Germany, Austria, and Czechoslovakia, were permitted entry into Britain without visas. Funds were raised, guarantors and foster families found, and the escapes organised, by a small but heroic group of volunteers, Jewish and Christian, in particular, Quakers. Later, limited government funds were made available.

Most of the Kindertransport children never saw their parents or families again. Without this scheme, these children would almost certainly also have died in the horrors of the ghettos and concentration camps. As it was, of the six million Jews who were murdered in the Nazi Holocaust, about a million and a half were children.

Although this particular story is about Jewish refugees, it should not be forgotten that other groups were also victims of the Nazi Holocaust: Gypsies; homosexuals; many with a mental or physical handicap; Slavs; socialists and others in the resistance; and anyone who tried to help or shelter Jews, including members of the Lutheran church, and numerous individual Catholic priests and nuns. And of course there were some ordinary people, like Karl's headmaster, and the Mullers' neighbour in the story, who had the courage to risk their lives for decency and humanity.

Millisle: the place

The small Jewish community of Belfast responded wonderfully to the needs of the young refugees who ended up in Northern Ireland. A Refugee Aid Committee was set up, and funds were raised by the communities of Belfast and Dublin, from the Central British Fund, and later from the Northern Ireland Ministry of Agriculture. Also in Belfast, a Committee for German Refugees was launched under the umbrella of, and with funding from, the Joint Christian Churches.

A hostel was established at Cliftonpark Avenue, Belfast, initially for a group of older religious refugees. When the Kindertransport children began arriving, nearly every Jewish family, and many non-Jewish families, took a child into their homes. In May 1939, the Refugee Aid Committee leased a derelict farm of about 70 acres, part of which had previously been used for bleaching damaged flax.

The Refugee Settlement Farm, or 'the Farm', as it was called, was situated close to the village of Millisle, County Down, on the Ards Peninsula, about 20 miles from Belfast. Up to 80 people, including the children, lived and worked on the Farm at any one time. In all, from the first arrivals in May/June 1938, to its closure in 1948, well over 300 adults and children are believed to have passed through it. The refugee children under the age of fourteen attended the local school, and many continued on to secondary schools, as Karl did in the story.

In October 1940, the Farm had 2 horses, 7 cows, 2,000

chickens, 16 acres of vegetables, and the rest in cereals. Crops included oats, barley, wheat, carrots, Brussels sprouts, cabbages, cauliflowers, potatoes, onions, turnips, and corn on the cob.

Recently, when I visited the farm, now privately owned, I received a warm welcome from the present owners, and a delicious Ulster tea like that in the story! I was shown around by Bobbie Hackworth (Bobbie Hackett in the story), a local historian who still lives in Millisle village. He attended school with the refugees, and played football with them, and is still in contact with some of them.

Although the wooden huts which housed the dormitories and the recreation room ('the rec') are no longer there, the old stone farmhouse (known as Ballyrolly House) remains, as does the large, twin-gabled structure built by the refugees themselves; this included the cow byre, with workshops and storage rooms above, where the refugees' suitcases and other items were kept.

The dunes on Millisle beach, where children played, known then as 'The Knowes', no longer exist. But you can still walk, as the refugees did, the three miles along the shore from Millisle to Donaghadee, although the cinema they visited is now the community centre. The Ballycopeland Windmill, just outside Millisle village, has been restored and, with the miller's house, is open to the public. It is the only complete windmill in County Down.

Millisle: the people

Karl Muller was partly inspired by Walter Hirsch, originally from Dresden, now living in London with his wife, a fellow-refugee from Millisle. However, Karl's character, thoughts, and his personal experiences, like those of other refugees in the story, are fictional. Walter Hirsch, and several other former refugees, now living mostly in the UK, USA and Canada, were generous with interviews, replies to my questionnaires, videos, diaries, short stories, photos and letters, and above all, with their memories.

A few of the former Farm residents still live in Northern Ireland, among them Edith Kohner. Now in her eighties, she provided me with detailed recollections of her years at the Farm, in which she, her husband and family played an important part.

Anton Senesh in the book is loosely based on the actual Farm manager, Eugen Pátriasz, a Hungarian refugee. Erwin Yakobi was indeed a saxophone player from Vienna, and according to the refugees, provided emotional support, especially for the younger ones. He died in the USA some time after the war.

Jack Freeman and the Gould family are fictitious, as are the Crawford family and Grace Doherty. However, several Ulster people employed on the Farm, who were crucial to its working, included a young woman who was in charge of the poultry.

Along with a few others (including 'the Postilion') and

some of the older refugees, all these adults played a part in the difficult job of welding this disparate group, of varying ages, from different countries, many of them children alone, many emotionally scarred, and all displaced, into a thriving, working farm community. The courage and determination of the refugees, both adults and children, helped them to survive, and, as Karl put it in the story, to 'make a new life'.

Several young people did travel from Dublin during the war, to work on the Farm during the summer, or for longer periods. Those in the story are fictitious, and the tensions I have described between the refugees and the Dubliners, were invented for the purposes of the story. In fact, those Dubliners I interviewed have warm and extremely happy memories of their time on the Farm.

Northern Ireland and the War

The Easter Tuesday Blitz in 1941 took Belfast by surprise. Throughout the winter of 1940-41, when British cities were being heavily bombed, Belfast remained untouched. In early April, there was a much smaller raid on Belfast. But for the most part, despite the taunts of Nazi broadcaster, Lord Haw Haw, that there would be 'Easter eggs for Belfast', most people did not believe the province would be a major target.

On the night of the raid, 16 April 1941, there was a cloudless sky and a full moon – a 'bombers' moon'. Belfast, largely unprepared, had few searchlights, inadequate shelters, only 22 anti-aircraft guns (augmented during the raid by the guns of HMS *Furious*, in Belfast Harbour for repairs), and one squadron of fighters.

Between one hundred and two hundred Luftwaffe bombers took off from bases in Northern France, and by dawn the next morning about 745 people in Belfast had been killed, and nearly 500 seriously injured. There was massive destruction, especially in residential areas, many of them overcrowded workers' dwellings. Whole streets of terraced houses, and quiet suburbs were destroyed. The giant York Street flax spinning mill (where Peewee's Granny used to work), caused huge devastation when it collapsed on the rows of little houses around it, home to the close communities of mill workers. In that incident alone, over 35 people, most of them related, died.

At the height of the raid, when the water mains had been punctured, communications cut off, and huge fires were burning out of control, a telegram was sent to Dublin via the railway telegraph service (telephone lines between North and South having been severed) requesting help. The Taoiseach, Eamon de Valera, was woken, and on his authorisation 13 fire engines and 70 men were despatched to Belfast from Dublin, Dun Laoghaire, Dundalk and Drogheda. This was a breach of Irish neutrality, but a most welcome gesture. The death and destruction witnessed by the volunteer firemen that day in Belfast, were long remembered by them.

A few bombs fell on that same night on other towns in the North, and on Newtownards Airfield, in which members of the Young Soldiers Battalion of the Inniskilling Fusiliers were killed, as happened to Wee Billy in the story.

Although Belfast experienced four Luftwaffe raids in all, including a later one in which much of the Harland and Wolff shipyard was destroyed, the casualty figures of the Easter Tuesday Blitz were among the highest of any city in Britain or Northern Ireland, in a single night. On that horrific night, people of all faiths did indeed work together and pray together as described in the story. The Belfast Blitz brought the reality of the war into the heart of the province, and remains one of the most dramatic and tragic episodes of the war in Northern Ireland.

The End of the Story

Most of the refugees remained at Millisle Farm until the end of the war, and some stayed on until it finally closed in May 1948. As they grew older, many joined the Pioneer Corps of the British Army, some left to get jobs, and others, with financial support from refugee organisations, went on to further education.

Only some time after the end of the war in 1945, did they finally learn what had happened to their families and loved ones. But that is another story.

Marilyn Taylor,
Dublin, 1999

ACKNOWLEDGEMENTS

I would like to thank most sincerely the following people and institutions. All of these provided generous and invaluable help and information, on all aspects of the book.

Ronnie Appleton, Jonathan Bardon, Edith Bown, Michael Brennan, Valerie Coghlan, Fiona and Cliona Eogan, Bobbie Hackworth, Walter Hirsch, Moshe Jahoda, Gerry Jayson, Walter Kammerling, Edith Kohner, Donal McCay, Rosemary Nicholl, Henry Solomon, Mervyn Solomons, Robert Sugar, Paul Symington, Liz Morris and pupils of Rathmichael National School, Annette O'Brien and Anne Doherty and pupils of St Louis High School, Theresa O'Kelly and pupils of Loreto College, Beaufort.

I would also like to express my appreciation to members of my family, Adam Taylor, Maryanne Taylor, Gideon Taylor and Debbie Kazis, and in particular to my husband, Mervyn, all of whom gave me practical help, and enduring and patient support during the (very!) long period of research and the writing of this book.

The author and the publisher would also like to thank the Northern Ireland Environment and Heritage Service and the American Jewish Joint Distribution Committee for permission to reproduce photographs. Extract from 'The Stolen Child' by W.B. Yeats courtesy of A.P. Watt Ltd. on behalf of Michael B. Yeats.

INSTITUTIONS

Northern Ireland

Belfast Education & Library Board

Linenhall Library, Belfast

Public Libraries: Newry, Donaghadee and Newtownards

North Down Heritage Centre, Bangor, County Down

Northern Ireland Environment & Heritage Service
(Marion Meek, Curator of Historic Buildings)

Regimental Museum, Royal Inniskilling Fusiliers
(Major G.E.M. Stephens)

South-Eastern Education & Library Board

Dublin

Dublin Corporation Libraries: Rathmines Library and
Terenure Library (in particular, librarian Eva Ndaba).

Jesuit Library, Milltown Park (Fr Brendan Woods, Irish
Library)

National Library of Ireland

South Dublin Libraries: Tallaght County Library and
Ballyroan Library

London

World Jewish Relief (Amy Zahl Gottlieb)

BIBLIOGRAPHY

Jonathan Bardon, *A Shorter Illustrated History of Ulster*

Brian Barton, *Belfast in the Blitz*

Causeway Magazine, Spring 1998

George Clare, *Last Waltz in Vienna*

Martin Gilbert, *The Boys;* also *The Holocaust*

Tony Gray, *The Lost Years: The Emergency in Ireland 1939-1945*

Robert Harbinson, *Song of Erne*

Maurice Hayes, *Sweet Killough Let Go your Anchor;* also *Black Pudding and Slim*

Norman Johnston, *Peace, War and Neutrality*

Bertha Leverton and Shmuel Lowensohn, *I Came Alone: Stories of the Kindertransports*

Elizabeth McCullough, *A Square Peg: an Ulster childhood*

Chris McGimpsey, *Bombs on Belfast*

Brian Moore, *The Emperor of Ice Cream*

Harold E. Smith, *Belfast newspaper articles on Millisle, 1939–1941*

Barry Turner, *And the Policeman Smiled*

THE JACKIE AND KEV TRILOGY
by Marilyn Taylor

COULD THIS BE LOVE?
I WONDERED

It begins with a look: but when Jackie actually meets the boy from the bus-stop, it's not so simple. Is Kev interested in her or not? Her friends are full of advice, but how can she tell for sure?

Romance isn't the only challenge for Jackie. At home there are money problems and her young brother's brush with the law. Why is life so easy in films and so complicated in real life, she wonders. Paperback £4.99/€6.34/$7.95

COULD I LOVE A STRANGER?

Daniel, a dark mysterious boy, comes to stay — when Jackie's boyfriend, Kev, is working abroad. Why is Jackie so attracted to Daniel? Is it simply the diary he shares with her, which documents the heart-rending story of a Jewish family in Nazi Germany and their attempts to escape to freedom?

Jackie has to make some difficult choices involving Daniel, Kev and her best friend, Deirdre. A dramatic event on a beach brings the conflict to a head. Paperback £4.99/€6.34/$7.95

CALL YOURSELF A FRIEND?

It's back to school and exams for Jackie. But when Bernie is knocked down by a drunken driver things begin to get very complicated – especially when Kev decides to take the law into his own hands. Can Jackie and Kev's relationship survive all the trauma?

Meanwhile, Andy the Hunk is back on the scene. Is he two-timing Deirdre, Jackie's best friend? The girls are determined to find out.

Paperback £4.99/€6.34/$7.95

Other Books from The O'Brien Press

ALLISON
Tatiana Strelkoff

When Karen meets Allison her world is turned upside down. What are these feelings she has for this girl? Can she trust her own heart? There is danger in being different. Can Karen overcome peer prejudice, parental opposition and the very real threat to her life from the school bully to remain true to herself and find happiness?

Paperback £5.99/€7.61/$8.95

SISTERS...NO WAY!
Siobhán Parkinson

Cindy does NOT want her Dad to remarry after her mother's death – especially not Ashling's mum. No way do these two want to become sisters! A flipper book, this story comprises the very different diaries of the two girls as they try to come to terms with the events unfolding in their lives.

Paperback £4.99/€6.34/$7.95

FRIEND OF MY HEART
Judith Clarke

Daz is in love with Valentine O'Leary, the biggest pig in Mimosa High School. Her brother William is in love with a girl he's never spoken to. Eleanor Wand, the music teacher, is in love with the headmaster. Everyone is in love with someone – and doing rather badly. Meanwhile, Daz's granny is searching for Bonnie, the long-ago friend of her heart. Will *anyone* be successful in the quest for lost friends and true love?   Paperback £3.99/€5.07

THE HEROIC LIFE OF AL CAPSELLA
Judith Clarke

Al Capsella wants to be cool, to fit in with the other teenagers in his neighbourhood. And part of fitting in is to be like all the others – to be 'normal'. But despite his heroic efforts, Al faces a crippling pair of obstacles: his PARENTS. Along with schoolmates like Louis, Al has his own plans for surviving the abnormal and embarrassing antics of parents, grandparents and teachers.   Paperback £3.99/€5.07

Send for our full colour catalogue